I0817815

HIBISCUS HOMICIDE

JASMINE WEBB

Chapter 1

"Get back here, you whore," Daniel Stockton shrieked at me as I launched myself toward the front gate of his expansive home. He chased me, but frankly, the dude didn't have a shot.

Fifty-four years old, a shade under six feet, and looking as if someone had dressed a snowman and given him a twenty-million-dollar home on Maui, Daniel was not going to catch me, even if the other day, I had gotten winded climbing up two flights of stairs.

Unfortunately for me, the front gate was probably a solid seventy or eighty yards from the front door. Now, if I were Usain Bolt, this wouldn't have been a problem. But no, I was Charlie Gibson, an almost-thirty-year-old with an affinity for nachos who thought the only thing worth running to was happy hour.

So as the gate began to close in front of me, I immediately knew I was never going to make it. I was going to be trapped on this property, and Daniel was going to catch me. And then? Who knew? He would probably try and hunt me for sport, like in that one Jean-Claude Van Damme movie my tenth-grade boyfriend made me watch with him. After all, that was the kind of money this place exuded.

Daniel Stockton was one of the richest men on Maui. He was a retired hedge fund manager who now lived in Makena, south of the posh resorts of Wailea, along a bumpy, borderline one-lane road that was so far away from civilization that very few tourists ever made it this far.

What was I doing here, you ask? Easy. I was robbing him.

Daniel's wife had hired me three weeks ago to find the overseas bank accounts she knew he was siphoning their money into, hiding it from her so that when she inevitably filed for divorce—as it turned out, in retirement, Daniel enjoyed not only sunshine but the company of prostitutes—he'd be able to keep her from getting her due.

Unfortunately for him, Daniel's wife, Denise, was a lot smarter than he gave her credit for. She had refused to be a simple housewife who turned a blind eye to her husband's infidelities, and when she found out what he had been doing, she leapt into action.

First, she hired a forensic accountant to go through the family's finances, the husband of a woman she knew from a country club back in New York. He was the one who had alerted her to the fact that there was money disappearing somewhere, and he couldn't track it. Then, Denise came to me.

Obviously, I put Dot on the case, but she had no more luck. Rosie, who knew a lot more about secret bank accounts and money laundering than either of us, wasn't surprised.

"You truly cannot understand just how important the secrecy of offshore banking is," Rosie said. "The Panama Papers that were released a few years ago barely even scratched the surface, and the journalist who leaked them was murdered shortly afterward. Even Dot isn't going to be able to hack into those banks easily. Not to mention, you need the account number and the bank name before you can even start your search. Otherwise, you're trying to find a needle in a haystack."

"Okay," I'd said, thinking pragmatically. "How do we get that number?"

"Well, it's probably in his home somewhere," Rosie mused. "Either that, or he might keep it in a safety deposit box. But my guess is it's closer than that."

"All right, cool. So, if I get that bank account number, Dot, do you think you can get access to it?"

"Please. Those uptight Swiss should stick to making watches and chocolates. Their banks have nothing on me."

Initially, the plan had been to get Denise to try and find the bank account number. After all, she lived in the home with Daniel. Unfortunately, he was a lot more careful than we thought, and he managed to keep his office closed to her at all times, and was worried that if she snooped around too much Daniel would get suspicious and try to kill her.

That was how I had ended up here in the Stockton family home. Rosie and I had found the number, no problem, after breaking into his office when he had gone out for the day. In the interest of keeping Denise's name out of it, we made sure she'd gone shopping for the day, too. Unfortunately, Daniel had returned home earlier than either of us expected. When we heard the creak of the gate at the front of the property opening, the two of us froze. I told Rosie to get out of here with the statement we'd found, hidden in a secret panel underneath Daniel's desk, and I'd distract him.

She'd immediately nodded and left the room, and knowing Rosie, she was probably halfway back to Kihei by now.

Of course, that left me to escape the clutches of the man now coming after me down the driveway. I had waited until he entered the house to show myself, making sure to leave a clear lane for me to run past him and out the front door. Once there, I sprinted across the looping driveway, past the covered patio that was bigger than my apartment, with a built-in outdoor grill. Past the in-ground pool, its perfect cyan water twinkling in the sunlight, surrounded by a white, eight-foot-high fence designed to keep prying eyes from having a look at the multimillion-dollar property behind it. It was probably also designed to keep the people being hunted by the owner on the grounds so he could find them.

No, that was ridiculous. The ultrarich hunting people for sport just could not be a real thing. Or so I told myself. If it was, I wouldn't last nearly as long as the Muscles From Brussels did.

Okay, it was time to stop thinking about bad action movies from the nineties and focus. I was still running toward the gate, even though the gap was now narrow enough that there was no way I'd get through it without being crushed to death. So I had to get over the wall somehow. It was made of lava rock but had been ground smooth enough that I didn't have a chance of climbing it.

There were a bunch of palm trees I could scale to jump over the top, but of course, that was ridiculous. I was well aware that I didn't have any of the skill sets required to shimmy up a palm tree.

I could stop and fight Daniel too. If I could knock him out, I could then grab his remote to control the gate and open it again. But of course, that was a very big if. And while I could outrun the guy, he had at least a hundred pounds on me, and I wasn't going to come out of a fight on the right side of things. I knew that. It was pointless to even consider it.

No, I had to escape over the fence somehow.

I immediately ran toward the right, over a lawn so perfectly manicured a round of golf could have been played on it. Then, I beheld a beautiful sight: the lava rock wall ended after about thirty yards and turned into a hedge. It would probably hurt, but I was pretty sure I could run through a hedge, Wile-E-Coyote style.

Besides, it was certainly a better option than being caught trespassing on Daniel Stockton's property. Best-case scenario: he'd call the cops, I'd spend the night in jail, and Zoe would have to bail me out because there was no way I'd be calling my mom in that situation.

"Hedge it is," I muttered to myself. I wasn't getting out of this without a few scratches, that was for sure. But hey, I'd rather look like I lost a fight with a raccoon than be arrested. Or hunted for sport.

I dared a look behind me to find that Daniel had stopped running after me. In fact, he was aiming a shotgun in my direction.

"Shit," I yelped, darting to the left as he pulled the trigger. A shot rang out, and if I hadn't already been panting for air, I would have held my breath, waiting for pain to course through me. But when, a second later, I didn't feel anything, I assumed he'd missed.

Those hedges couldn't come soon enough.

I didn't dare look back to see if he was going to shoot at me again, and I ran at full speed into the eight-foot-high hedge, closing my eyes and trying to do an awkward half-dive into the branches. I was trying to slice through the hedge instead of forcing my way through and making a Charlie-shaped hole in it.

I eventually scrambled through the leaves and branches and rolled onto the ground on the other side of the property. When I opened my eyes, I was on the grass, staring at Makena Road directly in front of me. Rosie was there, driving my neon-blue-and-black Jeep, Queenie. She flashed the lights at me, and I got up, slightly dizzy, staggering toward the vehicle.

Out of the corner of my eye, I could see the gate to Daniel Stockton's estate slowly sliding open once more, and I dove into the passenger seat of the car. Rosie peeled away, tires squealing, before I'd even gotten the door closed.

"He's coming after us," Rosie said, calm as anything. She glanced in the rearview mirror while I slammed the door closed and settled in my seat. I grabbed my seat belt and jammed it on, and not a second too soon.

The street along this part of Makena Road was not only narrow, basically one lane wide in total, but it had no shoulder whatsoever. Stone walls and shrubbery from the nearby mansions came to within a couple feet of the road, giving the whole area a boxed-in feel. And the road not only twisted and turned, but it rose and dipped. We passed a sign reading "no sight distance" as we approached a bump, and my heart leapt into my throat as Queenie got actual airtime going over the roll.

The Jeep slammed back down onto the ground on the other side, the vehicle's suspension getting a real workout, and I spun backward, trying to get a look at our pursuer.

Sure enough, Stockton was coming after us in an enormous white GMC Yukon that was, frankly, completely out of place on this island. He was gaining on us. I swallowed hard, but I knew that if anyone was going to get us out of this, it was Rosie.

But when I turned back to see the road ahead, another Jeep was coming toward us. It was newer than mine, late model, silver, and wide enough that there wasn't enough space for both of us.

Luckily, this road was full of small pullouts used for cars to pass each other, and while the other driver slammed on his brakes, Rosie yanked Queenie's wheel to the right then back to the left. We drifted at an angle over the dirt and gravel in the pullout. She swung the car back onto the road, and I looked back with a grin. The Jeep had stopped but was far enough into the lane that it blocked the Yukon behind it.

Stockton leaned on his horn, angrily trying to get the Jeep driver to move, and while the Jeep's reverse lights came on, I knew it was too little too late for Daniel Stockton.

Rosie wasn't about to take a lead like that and squander it. Sure enough, we soon reached the turnoff into Makena State Park, and Rosie was able to overtake a few dawdling tourists, putting even more distance between us and Stockton. We flew back along the dusty road north toward Kihei, and when I realized there was no way he was going to catch us, I let out a whoop of celebration.

"We did it!" I cheered. "Well, more accurately, you did it."

Rosie chuckled. "You gave me the opportunity to get out unseen. This was a team effort."

"Hold on a second. I never gave you the keys to Queenie." I patted down the pocket of my shorts and pulled out my car keys. My *only* set of car keys. "How on earth did you get her started?"

"You realize this is a 1993 Jeep, right? Hotwiring this thing is child's play. It took me five seconds, tops. Now, give me something with an actual alarm system and electronic security, and I'll have a slightly harder time."

"In this instance, I'm glad you didn't," I said, flashing my friend a smile.

Rosie returned it, pulling off onto one of the side roads to lose Stockton even more.

"Me too. I heard the shotgun, and I must say I was a little worried."

"Only Tasers manage to successfully hit me," I replied with a wink.

This made Rosie burst out laughing. "Come on. Let's get this information to Dot so she can do her thing."

Chapter 2

A few minutes later, Rosie pulled Queenie into one of the visitors' spots in Dot's apartment complex, and the two of us climbed the stairs to her place.

"You're going to want to put some antibiotic cream on those cuts," Rosie said to me, eyeing me up and down as we walked down the hall.

"It's that bad, huh?" I asked, knocking on the door.

Dot swung it open a moment later, took one look at me, and exclaimed, "You look like you just lost a fight with a raccoon."

"Don't you know there aren't any raccoons on this island?" I shot back.

"I'll get her some antibiotic cream," Rosie said, rolling her eyes as she walked past me and down the hallway toward the bathroom.

"I'd be willing to bet there's some nutjob out Hana way who smuggled a raccoon onto the island at some point and keeps it as a pet," Dot said. "But I don't think Daniel Stockton is the type."

"Definitely not," I agreed.

Rosie returned, handing me a tube of goo that I started applying to my scrapes.

"A raccoon might mess up his perfect manicured garden," I added.

"It might have guarded his home a bit better though," Rosie said, waving the sheet of paper we'd taken in the air. "We got this easy as pie, and we would have slipped out unnoticed if he hadn't come home earlier than we expected. That was unlucky, but there's always a risk when you're breaking and entering. Here's a statement from his bank."

"Oh, good," Dot said, taking the paper and heading to her computer. "This, I can work with."

"How long is it going to take you to hack into the bank?" I asked. I put the cap on the cream and handed it back to Rosie, who immediately unscrewed it and began rubbing cream on the spots I'd missed.

"Depends on the bank, really. Probably a few hours at the very least. I imagine there will be multiple layers of firewalls to get through. You should make yourself comfortable. We're probably going to be here for a while."

"Great," I said, plonking myself down on the couch. "Well, if that's the case, we might as well order some food. What are you in the mood for?"

"I'm good with anything," Dot said.

I turned to Rosie. "Do you have a preference?"

"Something Asian. Maybe Thai?"

"Works for me. I can go and pick it up."

I placed an order and, half an hour later, returned to find Dot still tapping away at the computer, her screen looking like something out of *Hackers*. Rosie assembled her a bowl of yellow Thai curry with a couple of spring rolls and brought it to her desk, but Dot was too engrossed in what she was doing to eat just yet.

Rosie and I grabbed bowls for ourselves and settled down on the couch, waiting for Dot to finish.

"Thanks for waiting for me at the house, by the way," I said with a grin. "I appreciate it. I'm not sure how things would have ended for me if you hadn't."

"Of course. I wasn't just going to leave you there. It's better he not know I was involved though."

"I agree. Although I suppose it was a risk. What if he had caught you?"

Rosie shot me a look. "First of all, he never would have caught me." She said it matter-of-factly, as if it were a given. "Secondly, my phone is set up to immediately back up everything I take a picture of to the cloud for exactly this reason. As soon as I got out of the house and to the car, I took a photo of the document and uploaded it. Had something happened to us, Dot still would have been able to access it, as I've given her the password to my account. That was why I knew it was safe to wait for you. The document would have made it to Dot no matter what happened to us."

"Wow," I said, impressed. "That's good thinking. But then, I guess that's normal for you."

"Just because technology has improved since the

sixties doesn't mean I haven't kept up with it," Rosie said with a wink. "Do you know how quickly the Cold War would have been over if we'd had today's technologies back then? Someone would have been texting photos of JFK to the *Washington Post* in the middle of the Cuban Missile Crisis."

"Well, I wouldn't really know. I wasn't born until after it ended," I said with a shrug.

"And that's the end of the conversation, because now I feel old," Rosie said. "Unlike Dot, who will never admit to it."

"Damn straight," Dot replied from her spot at the computer, her eyes never leaving the screen.

Rosie winked at me. "Being old means I get to eat whatever I want now, so I'm going to have another spring roll. Would you like one?"

"Yes, please," I said happily, pulling out my phone. I wanted to call Denise and give her an update on the situation, but I had a couple of Facebook notifications. Curious, I checked them first and found that Leslie and my mom had both tagged me in an article posted by a local Maui news site.

"Another tourist has been murdered, by the looks," I said.

Rosie raised an eyebrow. "No kidding."

"In Ka'anapali. It looks like they found his body early this morning. Some guy from New York named Rex Thunder. Seventy-six years old. Now that's a name."

"What did you say?" Rosie asked, snapping to attention.

"That if I wanted to be a guy with the coolest name ever, I'd want to be named Rex Thunder," I said with a grin.

"That's his name?" Rosie asked again, her voice curt.

"Yeah. Why? What's wrong?"

Rosie immediately stood up and began pacing. "It can't be. No way. Is there a photo of him?"

I scrolled through the article and shook my head. "Not on this news site. But I mean, I can look him up if you want. There can't be that many people out there with that name."

"Yes," Rosie said immediately. "Please do."

Rosie obviously didn't feel like giving out more information right now, so I just shrugged and began my search. I figured at seventy-six, he might be a bit too old to have many social media accounts out there, but the name was unique enough that I thought a simple Google search might get me a picture. Sure enough, when I searched "Rex Thunder New York" in Google images, a few results appeared. Fewer than I would have expected, but then I supposed Rex had lived most of his life before the internet was as prevalent as it was now.

Two pictures of one man dominated the search results. Lines abounded on his square face, and his deep brown eyes were large and expressive. He had a friendly smile, and I could tell just from the picture that this man was the kind of guy who could be friends with anybody.

"This guy?" I asked, handing Rosie my phone.

She looked at it and nodded. "Yes, that is him."

"How do you know him? Who is he?"

Rosie paused, took a deep breath, let it out, and then spoke. "His real name is Dmitri Ivanovich Volkov. We were engaged to be married."

Even Dot swung around to look at Rosie after that declaration.

"Rosemary Hunter, you never told me you were engaged."

"It was a lifetime ago," Rosie said with a casual shrug. "It never came up."

"Yeah, in the last thirty years, we've never once mentioned marriage," Dot said dryly.

"Oh no, Dot and Rosie are having a spat. What is the world coming to?" I asked with a grin.

"This isn't a spat," they both replied at the same time then turned to each other and laughed.

"Seriously though, I need to know this whole story," I said, turning to Rosie. "You were engaged to this guy? And he's actually Russian? Was he a spy like you?"

"Yes," Rosie replied, leaning into the couch. "I suppose I can tell you the whole story now. It no longer matters anyway. I met him in Petrograd, which we now call St. Petersburg, back in sixty-seven. I was barely nineteen years old and had just been recruited as part of a secret military program. Dmitri and I got along right from the start. It wasn't easy, working for this secret program. We were drawn to each other, and it didn't take long before our relationship became more than just friendly."

"Rosie and Dmitri, sitting in a tree," I sang.

"Well, a bunker designed to mimic a standard American town, anyway. There was a post office, and a soda shop, a McDonald's, and a Levi's store. It was actually kind of funny, the difference between where we trained and what our lives in America were actually like. But yes. He proposed to me six months after we met, in sixty-eight." A small smile flittered on Rosie's lips as her eyes glazed over slightly; she was lost in the memory. "Then, a week later, we were given our assignments. I was sent to Hawaii, while Rex was to go to Maryland."

"Oh, no," Dot muttered.

"Indeed. We knew instantly it was over. There would be no wedding. We would have no contact once in America; it was too dangerous. I couldn't write to him, he couldn't write to me, and we were thousands of miles apart and halfway across the ocean. So that was the end of that relationship. I moved on, of course. I lived my life, and it hasn't been a bad one, so I have no regrets. It's not as if we could have done anything differently anyway. If I'd gone after him, odds are I'd have ended up on the first plane back to Moscow if I was lucky, or with a bullet in my brain if I was unlucky. I'm not sad with the way my life ended up. I might never have married my first love, but that doesn't mean I didn't live a life full of joy and love all the same."

Rosie looked at Dot and me then, and I shook my head.

"Damn, that's hashtag goals right there," I said with a grin.

"Yes. So I'm not depressed about the direction my

life has taken, although I do occasionally think of Dmitri and wonder what he became. Was he out in the cold all those years? I suppose not, given this story."

"How did you know it was him?" I asked. "You knew before I showed you the picture."

A nostalgic smile spread across Rosie's face. "It was something he would say to me when we were training, in Petrograd. We were about halfway through our training, and one night in the middle of summer, the two of us left the bunkers and went out to lie in the grass. We stared at the stars, and we invented new lives for ourselves. Completely ridiculous lives. It started off with us just talking about where we'd be assigned. Dmitri wanted to go to New York City. He always thrived in urban environments. He thought the city was great because it was the perfect spot to speak with people, but you never really had to *know* anyone. He thought it would be a great place to have superficial relationships and that everyone important in America lived in New York. He'd be able to gather so much information. He'd be one of the most effective spies in the world. Novels would be written about his exploits. He'd be discussed in history classes. Or so he saw it."

Rosie chuckled. "Our dreams were very different, but at the same time, similar. I imagined that we would go to California. We would be assigned to a small town on the coast, where we would live as a husband and wife, travelling to the beach every weekend as we lived normal American lives. I would sneak secret messages in the pies I baked, and after a few years, they would lead to the downfall of the government. We'd be called home, and I'd be declared a hero and awarded the Order of Lenin in Red Square. Brezhnev himself would pin the medal to my chest, and I'd be as famous as Valentina Tereshkova, the first woman in space.

"As we kept talking, our fantasies became more and more elaborate, and they included names. I was going to be Eleanor Thunder, née Fernsby. It sounded very classy to me at the time. Named after the former First Lady herself. And of course, Dmitri was going to be Rex Thunder."

"And you figured there was no way that was a coincidence," I said, understanding.

"It couldn't be. Come on. What kind of person is *actually* named Rex Thunder? That's a name made up by a Russian child in the grass dreaming of glory."

"But you didn't take on the name of Eleanor Fernsby when you defected?" I asked.

"No. I didn't want to take any risks of being found, and I'd already spoken that name aloud, even though it was to someone who could presumably never find me. It was still too much of a risk, and I wouldn't do it. I invented Rosemary Hunter, taking common first and last names of the time. There were probably thousands of other women with that name around the country. I wouldn't stand out one bit. I wonder now..." Rosie trailed off, lost in thought.

"I wonder what he was doing on Maui," Dot said. "We need to find that out, at the very least."

"No," Rosie said suddenly. "No, we can't look into this at all. We have to let it go. Let him die."

"You do realize that he might not be on Maui by

accident, right? I know the Cold War ended thirty years ago, Rosie, but your ex-fiancé, who went through the same super-spy program as you back in Russia, just turned up dead on your doorstep."

"I know. I'll deal with it," Rosie said.

"Let us help," I implored. "I know you want to do this on your own, but Dot and I want to help you here. We can do the basic investigation. You know, ask questions that won't get a rise out of anybody. I'm an investigator. We can do it under the guise that I'm trying to drum up business. It makes sense, and your name doesn't have to come up at all. You won't be involved, you won't be dragged into this, and your secret won't be revealed."

Rosie paused, looking at the two of us. "You know, if this was thirty years ago, there's no way I'd say yes to bringing in anybody to help me get to the bottom of this. But I like to think that life experience has taught me it's all right to rely on your closest friends. So all right. Let's do this together. But if it looks like things are getting dangerous, I want the two of you out. Probably off this island. You have no idea what these people are capable of."

"I saw you snap a woman's neck like you were opening a jar of pickles. I know exactly what you're capable of," I said. "But it's settled. We're going to investigate, and find out what Rex Thunder was doing on this island, and if it somehow had anything to do with you."

I was really worried my friend was in danger.

Chapter 3

It only took about another half hour for Dot to finish hacking into the bank account and get all of the documents that Denise's lawyer would need to make sure the upcoming divorce would go her way. I forwarded them on to Denise, and Dot and I headed straight up to Ka'anapali to see what we could find out about Rex Thunder's murder, leaving Rosie in Kihei.

"I really had no idea she had been engaged," Dot said with a laugh as I pulled onto South Kihei Road, heading north.

"A woman like that, she's always going to have secrets."

"You're not wrong there. I don't pretend to know everything about her. But we've known each other a long time, and she's never told me about him. I'm not mad that she hasn't, of course. If she wants to keep something to herself, that's her right. In fact, I'm not even all that surprised. You know Rosie. She's always played everything close to the vest at the best of times. I'm the open book of the two of us."

"That's true. I even know you lived in Alaska at one point."

"I did. Chasing a man. Dumb idea. Never follow men, and never live in Alaska."

"Too many bears?"

"Too cold. You can piss out a walking stick in the winter. Not for me. No sir. And of course, it didn't help when Henry decided he was going to prove his manhood by getting into a fight with a grizzly bear. Spoiler alert: he lost."

"He *died*?" I asked with a gasp.

"No. But it made me realize how much of an idiot he was and how much of an idiot I was for leaving Maui for a place where the mosquitoes can pick you up and carry you off."

I snorted as I turned off the highway. Even though it was early afternoon on a Tuesday in late September, and most of the summer tourists had gone home, there was still virtually no chance I was going to get a free parking spot anywhere in Ka'anapali. They were just too rare.

Instead, I parked at Whaler's Village, the local mall. "This way, we have to get some ice cream when we're done so we get our parking validated," I said to Dorothy.

"I like the way you think."

We exited the mall on the beach side and found ourselves on the Ka'anapali Beachwalk, a well-maintained boardwalk that stretched for five miles along

Ka'anapali Beach, offering tourists and locals alike an easy option for strolling along one of the most gorgeous beaches on all of Maui.

At the far north end was Black Rock, a popular spot for swimming and snorkeling by tourists and where the more adventurous *keiki* climb to the top of the rocks and jump off into the water below.

In Hawaiian lore, Black Rock—called *Pu'u Keka'a* in the Hawaiian language—was believed to be the spot where, after death, souls departed the earth and crossed over into the spirit world. The last ruling chief of Maui, King Kahekili, was known for his cliff-jumping prowess, and Pu'u Keka'a was reportedly one of his favorite spots from which to leap into the water. This was considered an amazing feat, since only someone with very powerful energy, or *mana*, could jump from a place where souls crossed over and return unharmed.

It looked as if Rex Thunder's spirit didn't have too far to go to cross over, either. As soon as we reached the boardwalk, it was obvious from the crowds that the body had been found to the north, toward Black Rock. I motioned with my head to the right, and Dot and I headed in that direction, following everyone else.

To our left was some greenery, mainly low-rise bushes and flowers, giving everyone walking along a view of the beautiful beach a little bit further. Interspersed among them were larger trees, mainly palms, banyans, and banana trees, offering shade as the occasional respite from the sun's warm rays. Ka'anapali Beach was one of the longest, most beautiful beaches on the island, and it was no surprise that when the powers that be had decided to turn Maui into a tourist destination in the seventies and eighties, they'd focused their attention along this strip. The yellow-white sand sparkled in the sunlight as if studded with diamonds. Soft waves lapped rhythmically against the shore, the azure ocean inviting and calm. The happy cries of children were quickly carried away by the warm breeze. Heads dotted the water as people swam, the tips of snorkels visible above the surface, while farther out, a couple people paddleboarded casually along.

I shuddered at the idea of getting onto one of those death traps again.

On our right, Dot and I walked past resort pools and restaurants, the warm tones of the ukulele playing in the background as onlookers enjoyed an afternoon drink at the bars that offered unmatched views of the water.

Loungers that overlooked the path—and the beach beyond—were filled with relaxing holidaymakers, sunglasses over their eyes as the sun beat down upon them, and I knew more than one of them would inevitably underestimate the sun's rays and head back to their rooms looking like freshly cooked lobsters.

As we got farther north, however, we reached the growing crowd that I was sure would be interested in checking out the crime scene. Eventually, we arrived at a wall of people, and I stood on my tiptoes, trying to see how far we were from the police barricade that would be keeping people back.

"It looks like we're about ten, maybe fifteen people back," I said to Dot with a shrug.

"Right. Well, watch how it's done." Dot shook her arms and legs a little bit, as if she was an athlete getting ready to get out there on the field, and charged through the crowd. "Coming through. Excuse me, make room. Just because I'm short doesn't mean I won't kick you if you don't let me pass."

I smiled to myself as I followed closely behind Dot. She snaked through the crowd expertly, and the next thing I knew, we were pressed against the yellow police tape, looking at the crime scene.

Not that there was all that much to see. The body had evidently already been removed, although going by the location of the crime scene technicians, it was obvious where it had been found.

This section of the path was one of the few parts that was fully covered on both sides. For about a thirty-foot-long stretch, tall trees created a canopy overhead, creating a makeshift tunnel. It was dark and ominous looking beneath the branches. Also, it was the perfect place along this stretch to commit a murder without being seen.

On the right-hand side were some bushes dotted with hibiscus flowers. This had to be where the body had been found. A few of the white hibiscus flowers were stained red with blood, and a few of the leaves were now rust colored as well.

On top of that, a crime scene photographer moved about the scene, pausing occasionally for a second, like a buzzing bee moving from flower to flower only, instead, moving from shot to shot.

I looked around, half expecting to see Jake

Llewelyn somewhere, but I didn't. I had to admit that my heart dropped slightly from disappointment at the realization that he wasn't here. It made sense, of course. Jake worked out of the police station in Kihei; he wouldn't be called in to investigate a murder up here in Ka'anapali. And I wasn't quite ready to acknowledge what that disappointment meant, so I pushed it aside and instead focused on the scene.

Almost everyone around me had their phones out, taking photos and videos to share with friends and family on Instagram and Snapchat.

I went to Maui and all I got was a glimpse of a crime scene and a piña colada.

I looked around a little bit more to see if anyone looked out of place, but no. There wasn't much to glean from this scene.

"Notice anything?" I asked Dot.

"Nothing especially useful. I think he was killed in the hibiscus bushes, but that's all I can tell. I can't see anyone who looks especially broken up by his death, but then, they'd be unlikely to be out here, wouldn't they?"

"We need to get some details about what happened," I muttered, looking around. "Come on, let's get out of here."

Dot and I worked our way back through the crowd, and when we came out the other side, my eyes landed on a small open-air restaurant. I motioned for Dot to follow me, and we headed over to it, taking a couple of seats at the bar. The décor was tiki themed; the stools on which we sat were upholstered in bright hibiscus patterns, and the open tables on the patio were protected from the sun by thatched umbrellas. Tiki torches dotted the exterior, and behind the bar were a number of retro photos of Maui in the fifties and sixties.

"Hey there. What can I get started for you?" the bartender asked. In his twenties, with shoulder-length sandy blond hair and blue eyes, he looked like the quintessential surfer, and I was sure he'd have been out on the water this morning before his shift. The small tattoo on the inside of his wrist that read "Eddie Would Go" confirmed that he was, in fact, a surfer.

"I'll have a mai tai, and she'll have a Diet Coke, since she's driving," Dot said, ordering for me.

The guy looked over at me to confirm, and I nodded.

"Coming right up," he replied happily.

I looked around the restaurant. About three-quarters of the tables were occupied, and there were a couple other people at the other end of the bar. Another older woman took a seat two down from me, opened a well-used paperback, and began to read.

A moment later, the bartender slid two drinks over to Dot and me and went to take the woman's order. When he returned, Dot grabbed his attention.

"So, a bit of excitement happening out there today, isn't there?" she said, motioning with her head in the direction of the crowd. "I hear someone was murdered."

"That's the word going around," the barkeep replied. "They found him a few hours ago, just after my shift started. The poor woman who found him actually ran here for help after calling 9-1-1. I don't think she realized he was dead."

"Oh?" Dot asked. "Did you see the body?"

"No. I figured someone had to take care of her before the police arrived. She was in a really bad state. Shaking, crying, that sort of thing. When I realized what had happened I sent the manager, Katie, over to make sure no one got close to the body until the police showed up, and I got the woman some water and made sure she was okay."

"Did she tell you what happened?"

The bartender looked between us, and I reached into my pocket and pulled out a business card that I'd had made. "I'm a private investigator. I have a client who knew the victim and is interested in knowing about how he died. We're not reporters looking for a scoop or tourists trying to get a story."

"Right. I knew you looked familiar. You're the one who was on TMZ a few months back, working for Marion Hennessey."

"Yeah, before she got arrested for faking her own murder," I replied.

"That's the one. Okay. I'll help you. The woman said it looked like someone had hit the man's in the head. She said there was blood everywhere. Blood all over the flowers. That was what she kept repeating. 'Those beautiful flowers, there was blood on the flowers.' She obviously had a huge shock. I hope she gets help."

"Did she tell you how she happened to come across the body?" Dot asked.

"Not directly, but I overheard her telling the police the story. They came by and took her statement here, and I just happened to be close enough to overhear what she was saying."

Dot tapped her nose knowingly.

The bartender gave a slightly embarrassed smirk. "Hey, you can't be a good bartender if you're not a good listener. Anyway, she came out this way around nine. She was staying at the Sheraton and wanted to walk down to the mall to get some more sunscreen, as she'd run out of the reef-safe stuff she'd brought from home. She was walking along the path, admiring the flowers, and noticed the white hibiscus flowers with red on the petals. She looked more closely at them, thinking it was weird, and that was when she saw the body. There were two sets of independent hedges along there, and the body was shoved between them, so it was covered by all the shrubbery. I heard her yelp. I thought it came from the beach, and I didn't think much of it, but about a minute later, she came running over here, her phone in her hand. She had called the police."

"And your manager went to see the body?"

The bartender nodded. "Yeah. You're welcome to speak to her if you think it'll help, but I don't think she saw much. She was mostly just trying to keep people away. The cops got here quickly too. The first ones arrived within about three or four minutes of the woman calling them."

"Did you know the victim?" I asked.

The bartender shrugged. "Wouldn't have a clue. I never saw the body."

"Right." I pulled out my phone and found the picture of Rex Thunder that I'd showed to Rosie earlier. I flipped my phone around.

The bartender looked at it and nodded. "Oh, yeah, that guy. I do know him, actually."

"How often has he been here?"

"I don't know. A handful of times?"

"Did he tell you why he was on the island?"

"His daughter's wedding. That's horrible, isn't it? She's supposed to be getting married on Friday. Right on the beach. That poor family. They're all here. His wife, three kids, the fiancé's family. And of course, all their guests. I gathered they're loaded, though he didn't say so. But I got the impression he paid for everything. Usually that type, they stay down in Wailea, but he said his daughter and her fiancé had their first vacation here in Ka'anapali, and that's where they wanted to have their wedding, right there on the beach."

"How long had he been on the island?" I asked.

"Only a couple of days, I think. Maybe not even that. He complained about the jet lag from the six-hour time difference and started telling me about the things he was planning on doing while he was here after the wedding."

"Great, thanks," Dot said.

The bartender nodded then moved on to serve some of his other patrons.

Dot turned to me. "So, what do you think?"

"Well, on the bright side, if his daughter was

getting married here because she and her fiancé love this island, the odds of this being something to do with Rosie are pretty low," I said in a hushed whisper, making sure we wouldn't be overheard.

"I agree. It doesn't sound like he was here to look for her. It could have just been a coincidence. But then, you never know with those super-spy people, do you? I'm going to see if I can find his email account and hack into it. The hotel he's staying at should have it on record if he's paying for everything."

"Right. Good plan. I think we can go back to Rosie for now and tell her not to worry. So, this guy Rosie was engaged to has a family," I said slowly. "She never married, but I guess this guy moved on."

Dot snorted. "Of course he did. Men are always that type. He wasn't going to pine for Rosie forever. But then again, I don't think she did, either."

"No?"

"Well, you've met her. Does she seem like the pining type to you? No, I think she would have married if she'd found someone she loved. But look at her history. I think the thing she loved most in the world was freedom. Do you really think she would have been happy tied to a man?"

"That's a good point."

"Besides, it was a different time back then. I know it's hard for you youngsters to understand these days, because things have changed so much. But up until the seventies, and into the eighties even, if a woman was married, in a lot of ways she was still considered the property of her husband. It wasn't until 1974 that a woman in the United States could apply for a single credit occupation without having a man there to cosign for her. And that's just the law. There was a lot more pressure back then for a woman to conform to her husband's opinions. Can you really picture Rosie being happy in that kind of situation, especially given her past?"

I shook my head. "No, not really."

"Rosie's true love is America," Dot said with a wink. "As far as I'm concerned, the day she settled on Maui permanently is the day she got married, and she's never had a better partner."

"That's a fantastic way of putting it."

Dot finished up her mai tai, abandoning the straw and throwing back the last sip, and I left a fifty for the bartender to cover the drinks and the information he'd given us. I figured it was worth the extra to keep this guy on our side, and if he heard anything else, he'd be more willing to let us know if he knew we were happy to pay for the information.

Hopefully, it wouldn't be long before we found out for sure that Rex Thunder's trip didn't have anything to do with Rosie, and it was just a coincidence that he had been murdered on the same island where his ex-fiancée Russian spy now lived.

Chapter 4

Dot and I left the restaurant. The crowd attempting to have a look at the crime scene had grown. Word was getting around. Instead, we walked in the other direction along the path, back toward the car.

"Grab an ice cream for the road?" Dot suggested as we reached Whaler's Village once more.

With our treats—and validated parking—in hand, we headed back to the parking lot. We had just reached Queenie when the old woman who had been sitting next to me at the bar appeared out of nowhere, pointing a gun in our direction.

I was so shocked I dropped my ice cream.

"Either one of you move, you die," she said matter-of-factly.

I heard the sound of a gun cocking, and Rosie stepped out from behind the truck next to us, pressing a revolver to the other old lady's head. "You first."

The woman pressed her lips together. She was on

the taller side, probably about five foot seven or so, slim, with a round bob and wispy bangs that softened her square face. Her hair was ash blond and so natural looking I genuinely couldn't tell if it had come from a salon. She looked to be in her seventies, but she carried herself, well, she carried herself like Rosie.

"All right, put it down, nice and easy," Rosie ordered in a calm, steady voice. "Then we're all going to have a little chat like grown-ups, with our guns put away. We can do that, can't we?"

"Who are you?" the woman snapped, but she lowered her weapon.

"Safety on," Rosie said.

The woman paused but then complied with a sigh. "I've done my part. Now you do yours," she said, turning to face Rosie's gun head-on.

Rosie gave a curt nod and dropped her arm to her side before quickly tucking her revolver into the waistband of her pants.

"So," the woman said as if she hadn't just held a gun to my head. "What's your name?"

"You first," Dot said, still eating her ice cream.

I looked dejectedly down at mine, which was melting into a puddle on the hot asphalt.

"I'm Heather Thunder, Rex's wife," the woman said.

"Your real name," Rosie said.

"Heather Thunder *is* my real name."

"We both know your real name died on a plane between Moscow and JFK," Rosie replied. "But you have one, and it's not that."

"Who are you?" Heather snapped. "Did you finally get to him? Are you with the secret service the Russians are running now? Are you going to blow my brains out too, make it look like a murder-suicide?"

"Relax," Rosie said. "I'm not going to kill you. Not unless you give me a good reason to, anyway."

"She made me drop my ice cream. I think that counts as a good reason," I pointed out.

Rosie shot me a look.

"Why were you asking about Rex?" Heather asked.

"How did you find us? You obviously followed us into the restaurant," I replied.

Heather scoffed. "I was watching the crowd. Every single person there was taking photos to post on their social media except for you and your friend. The two of you were obviously looking for clues, looking for answers. So I followed you to the restaurant and listened in on your conversation with the bartender. You claim to be a private investigator, but no one from Rex's family has hired you. So who are you, really?"

"An interested third party," Rosie replied.

"You're not with the Russians?"

"No. Why do you think the Russians were after Rex? He was your husband, yes?"

"That's right. And because I've had one eye open for decades, since we defected, worried at every moment that someone would recognize us. That the wrong people would finally discover our true identities and that we'd be eliminated. Even just saying the words out loud to you right now is terrifying, but I don't have a choice, do I? And you're not surprised by this, anyway. Why not? You obviously know about my situation. Who are you? CIA? FBI?"

"Neither," Rosie replied. "Now, let's all calm down. There are too many questions floating around, and you're certainly asking a whole lot of them for someone who isn't in control right now. So let's sort things out, one question at a time. You don't *know* that the Russian government is after you, is that right? And Rex really was here for a family wedding? That's it? There was no ulterior motive?"

"No. No, there was nothing. Our daughter Melissa is getting married this Friday. That's why we're here. We haven't had anything to do with Russia for decades."

"All right. In that case, I apologize for the disturbance, and I'm sorry for the loss of your husband."

"Thank you," Heather said, looking slightly surprised. "But… is that it then? You're really just going to leave? What does any of this have to do with you?"

"Nothing. Nothing at all. It was just a miscommunication. I recommend you forget you ever met any of us and go about your day."

Heather's brow furrowed. "I don't even know your names."

"Let's keep it that way."

Heather took a couple steps back. "Are you really a private investigator?" she asked me.

"Yes."

"Would you investigate Rex's death if I hired you?"

"Absolutely not," Rosie replied. "We're going nowhere near this case."

Heather's eyes widened. "I get it! You're one of us." She rattled off something in what had to be Russian.

To her credit, Rosie didn't even blink. "I have no idea what you just said. Go. Mourn your husband. And don't draw a gun on my friends ever again, or it'll be the last thing you do."

"I'm serious about investigating his death," Heather replied. She pulled a card from her pocket and handed it to me. "If you change your mind, let me know. There's something fishy going on here, and I don't like it. There's no reason for anyone to kill Rex." With that, Heather turned and left.

Rosie watched her carefully, and it wasn't until she was well out of sight that she finally turned back to us. "Well, that certainly wasn't what I expected."

"Nothing is ever what I expect when you're around," I replied. "What are you doing here, anyway? Where did you come from? I thought this was supposed to be something Dot and I were going to investigate on our own."

"It was, but I was worried all the same. And as it turned out, my suspicions were correct. It turns out Rex married another Russian. And he has a family now. Ah, such is life. I am happy for him, that he got everything he wanted from this world. It never could have worked between us anyway."

"What did Heather mean by 'there's something fishy going on here'?" I asked.

"I don't know, and I'm uncomfortable with it,"

Rosie said, her mouth pressed into a hard line. "Heather is obviously worried about something. But the question is whether her fears have any basis in reality. She mentioned that she's been looking over her shoulder for decades, so perhaps she is seeing ghosts where there aren't any."

"But you're concerned there's something to it," I said.

Rosie nodded. "I don't like this situation being so close to home. I don't like that Dmitri was here; I don't like that there's another former Soviet spy on this island who just tried to get me to reveal my identity to her; I don't like any of this. It could all just be a coincidence. It could be a run-of-the-mill murder, an outburst by someone under pressure from the wedding. It's possible we're all just on edge because we're all worried about involvement by lettered government agencies, and that they don't have anything to do with this. But if they do, I need to know."

"So we've got to investigate this," I said.

Rosie sighed. "I was really hoping we'd be able to stay out of this. I want to be linked to Rex Thunder as little as possible. What an idiot, choosing a name that sticks out so much. And one he'd come up with in Russia, no less. I know I was the only one he told, but still. It's the principle of the thing. But that was Dmitri. Anyway, yes. I'd like to hire you, Charlie."

"Done. I'll solve this murder, and all it'll cost you is a replacement for that ice cream I dropped."

Rosie chuckled. "It sounds like you had a real emotional attachment to it. All right. We'll get you a replacement, and then you can start investigating. I want to stay out of this as much as possible though."

"Just like you were supposed to stay out of this and let Charlie and me handle this first part?" Dot asked with a smile.

"Yes, well, it turns out it was a good thing I was here, wasn't it?"

"I can't argue with that logic," I replied.

Ten minutes later, with a second cup of ice cream in my hand, I pulled out of the parking lot and back onto the Ka'anapali Parkway, the extra-wide, extra-smooth road that wound its way between the golf course and the resorts. Using my knees to steer Queenie, I took a bite of ice cream while stuck behind a tourist doing five miles an hour.

Suddenly, red and blue lights flashed in my rearview mirror. Great. I was totally going to get ticketed for driving with my hands off the wheel, even though the idiot in front of me was driving so slowly my little dog, Coco, could have kept up with him on one of her walks. How was that fair?

But no, at a closer look, this wasn't the police. At least, none I'd ever seen before. It was a convoy of three huge black SUVs that could not have looked more out of place here on Maui.

"Feds," Rosie muttered, glancing in the side mirror as I pulled over to let them pass. The clueless tourist in front of us didn't seem to notice them, and the SUVs rolled two wheels up onto the median strip between lanes to pass the car in front.

"They sure like to be inconspicuous, don't they?" Dot said. "What are they doing here?"

"I mean, I'll give you one guess," I said dryly.

"Sure, but why call in the feds? I think Heather was right. There's something going on. The FBI doesn't come and investigate a run-of-the-mill murder."

"And I need to keep my head down as much as possible," Rosie said as the SUVs turned off into the parking lot that led to a beach-access path that came out at the crime scene. "With the arrival of federal agents, I agree. I think there is certainly more to Dmitri's death than meets the eye."

We drove slowly past where the SUVs had pulled off, and sure enough, a handful of people in navy-blue windbreakers with FBI written in huge yellow letters on the back were exiting the SUVs, which had parked in the middle of the road. Even the FBI couldn't find a parking spot in Ka'anapali. I continued past, not wanting to draw attention to us. At the roundabout at the end of the street, we did a U-turn then headed back the way we'd come, turning onto Kekaa Drive to get to Honoapiili Highway.

Rosie was tapping her fingers on the edge of the door, staring out at the ocean. I glanced in her direction. "It's going to be okay," I told her.

"I've lived in this country as an American for decades. I took every conceivable precaution. I can count on one hand the number of people I've told my true identity to. And yet my ex-fiancé shows up on this island and winds up dead, with the FBI here within hours? No, that's not a coincidence, and I don't like that it's happened here. It's too close to me, and I need to know if I'm in danger."

I wanted more than anything to tell Rosie that she was fine, that she was almost certainly overthinking things. But Rosie wasn't the type to panic needlessly, and if she was worried, it was with good reason.

"Okay," I said. "First things first. I need a legitimate reason to investigate this murder that doesn't involve Rosie. I'm going to call Heather back. She seemed open to the idea of hiring me. If she's willing to do that, at least I can go around and ask questions without raising too many red flags. That will keep Rosie out of it, while still allowing us to get answers."

"Secondly, Rosie needs to *actually* stay out of it instead of telling us she's going to and then following us in secret," Dot said.

"I think we both know that's not going to happen," Rosie said, turning to shoot Dot a wry smile. "If this case has something to do with Dmitri's former life as a spy, then I need to be involved. But I'll do it from the shadows. I know how to be subtle. It's my specialty. It's just not yours."

"Okay, that's fair enough," Dot replied. "You know what you're doing. We're not going to pretend to tell you what to do, but if you need anything from us, you let us know. We will do everything under the sun to keep you safe, and to keep your true identity a secret."

"Absolutely," I confirmed.

I didn't know what was going on with Rex Thunder's death, but I was going to get to the bottom of it if it was the last thing I did.

Chapter 5

I dropped Dot and Rosie off at Dot's apartment building—Rosie promised she had a friend who was going to bring her CR-V back from Ka'anapali later on today—then headed back to my own place, which I shared with my best friend, Zoe Morgan.

Zoe was a doctor who worked the emergency room at the hospital on Maui. Tall, half Black, with natural hair that was currently styled in a mini afro that framed her face beautifully, Zoe was gorgeous both inside and out.

When I got home, she was reading a book on the couch with Coco resting against her, a glass of water and a bag of tortilla chips and some salsa on the coffee table.

"Afternoon," Zoe greeted me. "Did you get the bank account details off that rich guy?"

"Sure did. He tried to shoot me, but luckily, he missed."

Zoe raised an eyebrow. "You do realize you left Seattle so you'd get shot at *less*, right?"

"I know. But to be fair, I didn't realize he had a gun."

"This is America. Always assume that everyone has a gun."

"A very good point."

"I'm glad you weren't shot, at least. And you got the bank account number. Did Dot get the details yet?"

"Yes. They've been sent to Denise, and to her lawyer, and Daniel is about to find out that if you want to divorce your wife so you can get some action on the side, it's going to cost you. And then, almost immediately, we got another case. Rosie's ex-fiancé, from when she was training to be a spy in Russia, was killed in Ka'anapali today."

Zoe turned to me, concern etched all over her face. "What was he doing here? Is Rosie okay? Was he trying to find her?"

"She's fine for now. We're obviously investigating though, and trying to keep her out of it. So far, we haven't found any sign that he might have known Rosie was on the island. I don't think it had anything to do with her, but I do think there's more to this story than meets the eye. We even saw the FBI arrive on the scene. They don't just show up to something they think is an ordinary old murder."

"No," Zoe said, pressing her lips together.

"So there's something going on, and we're going to look into it just in case. Anyway, how's the ER? Lots of things stuck up butts?"

Zoe chuckled. "Not recently. I ran into Olivia, the woman who fixes up your Jeep."

"Oh yeah? Is she okay?"

"She's fine. She had a little bit of a mishap with… well, she explained it to me, but I didn't understand it. I know more about the inside of people than I do the inside of cars. But it was nothing a dozen stitches, a prescription for antibiotics, and a recommendation to take it easy for a few days couldn't fix. She asked me to ask you to call in and see her when you were next up her way. She's having trouble with her phone so she couldn't text you."

"Cool. I can do that. I'll go up there in a bit. I want Olivia to make sure Queenie's none the worse for wear anyway after Rosie had to gun it to get us away from Daniel Stockton. Did you know you can get air time off those humps on the road down there?"

Zoe grimaced. "It doesn't surprise me. I hate driving down there. Sometimes the beaches at that end of the island get great waves though."

"I like how you go out every morning and risk being eaten by a shark, and yet you dislike the bumps on the road."

"Do you know how much higher the odds are of getting into a car accident than of being attacked by a shark?" Zoe replied.

"Well, given as in this very apartment complex there are no people who have been severely injured in a car accident and one person who lost a leg to a shark, I think the shark attack is higher."

"This is why anecdotes don't count as data."

"It's also why I don't go in the ocean unless I absolutely have to."

"You're missing out. There's a whole amazing world under there."

"The world up here is crazy enough. I don't feel the need to add to it by exploring the depths of a place that has whales the size of a skyscraper, multiple species of sharks, long fish that electrocute you, and to top it all off, spiders."

Zoe laughed. "You forgot about the vampire squid."

"I didn't know that was a thing, and I don't think I want to know any more than what you've already said. Anyway, you're only proving my point."

"Fair enough. You don't have to love the ocean. Though I think you're probably the only kid to ever be born and raised on Maui who avoids it at all costs."

"The ocean killed Steve Irwin."

"A sting ray killed Steve Irwin."

"In the ocean."

"There are fluke accidents on land too, Charlie. You could get hit by a bus tomorrow."

"Not me. My reflexes are too good. If I'm going to die, it's going to be because I pet something fluffy that I shouldn't have petted."

Zoe snorted, then threw a tortilla chip at me. I ducked, but not before it hit me in the forehead. "Yeah, your reflexes are awesome."

"That's not fair, I wasn't expecting it. Anyway, are you working tonight? I can grab some dinner on the way back from Olivia's. I might have to run out quickly, though, if I hear anything about my case. Or if I get an update from Denise or her lawyer. You never know what might come up."

"I'm off tonight but working early tomorrow morning. It's too bad; it's looking like there might be a nice surge on the northern beaches in the morning, so I was hoping to catch some waves. Oh well."

"That's another reason I don't surf: I like sleeping in, and the best waves are during prime sleeping hours."

"Go through medical school and residency, and you'll learn that you don't really need as much sleep as you think you do," Zoe said with a grin. "And also that you can get up at any hour of the night."

"Yeah, the lack of sleep is definitely why I never went that route," I joked. "Okay, I'll come back with food at some point."

"Enjoy," Zoe said with a wave, going back to her book. Coco was still snoring away on the couch next to her when I left.

It was a gorgeous afternoon to drive with the top down, and before I pulled out onto the main street, heading toward the highway, I dialed Heather Thunder and put the phone on speaker.

"Hello?" she answered on the second ring.

"Hi, Heather. It's Charlotte Gibson here, but you can call me Charlie. We met this morning, when you put a gun to my head."

"Charlie. I was hoping to hear from you. No hard feelings about that, I hope."

"None at all. I was thinking about your offer and

wondering if you're still willing to hire me to find the person who killed your husband."

"Yes. I would be very appreciative if you could. The FBI has taken over his case, and in my experience, well, let me just say I don't trust that they are going to do right by him. I also believe my husband had secrets he kept even from me. They could be important, and I want you to find them. I believe that I can trust you. I don't know who the women with you were, but I've relied on my instincts to get me this far, and they haven't failed me yet. I feel like you're my best shot at getting answers. Real answers. I need to know what was going on, not only for Rex, but for my own safety going forward."

"I'll do my best to get them for you."

"If you need anything, let me know. I have a lot of resources available. Find the person who killed my husband, Charlie. And should you come across anything else… well, I won't speak of it over the phone. We must meet in person. I don't want it to be here. I can't have it be anywhere I might be spotted. Where can I meet you?"

"Do you have a car?"

"Yes."

"In that case, meet me tomorrow morning at six at the food truck parking lot in Kihei. There's a place to get coffee, but most people at that hour use the drive-through, so we'll have some privacy. It's located on Piikea Avenue."

"I'll be there," Heather said. "Tomorrow at six. Thank you, Charlie."

"Not a problem. I'll do my best to get you the answers you're looking for."

I pressed the red button on my phone to end the call and drummed my fingers against the steering wheel as I headed toward Olivia's home. At least now that was sorted out. I was working for Heather officially. Unofficially, I was going to be keeping Rosie in the loop when we saw how things progressed. Why was Rex Thunder here? Was the wedding just a pretense to get onto the same island as Rosie? Had he seen her image somewhere and recognized her from fifty years ago? Was he still working for the Russian government somehow? Was Heather involved in it as well? Was this all just a trap? Was someone going to come after Rosie? Or did we have this all wrong, and it really was just a normal murder, with a normal motive?

Yeah, I had way too many questions and exactly zero answers right now. I needed to meet with Heather and hopefully get a bit of a feel for this case, but that wouldn't be until tomorrow. I needed tonight to meet with Olivia. And then I could check in with Denise to make sure she didn't need anything else. After all, I was sure she would have met with her lawyer straight away. She'd texted me while we were up in Ka'anapali, thanking me for the files, but I wanted to confirm with her that the job was done.

Olivia lived on West Waikapo Road, off the highway, just a few miles south of Kahului. Gravel crunched beneath the tires as I pulled into her driveway, immediately greeted by her Rottweiler, Egg

McMuffin, who was the sweetest dog known to man. And also the drooliest.

"Hey, friend," I said to him as I was accosted while stepping out of the car. I gave him a quick pat on the butt as he wagged his entire rear end in hello before dropping a slobber-covered tennis ball at my feet. I picked it up and lobbed it as far as I could down the yard, and Egg went running after it, his four long legs lumbering behind him like an awkward teenager.

Olivia was in the open garage, her overall-covered legs sticking out from beneath a ten-year-old 4Runner, muttering under her breath as the occasional clang of metal on metal rang out from under the car.

"That doesn't sound good," I called out.

Olivia rolled the creeper out from beneath the chassis, pulled herself upward into a seated position, and flashed me a grin. "It's a beautiful sound, actually. I love working on Toyotas. They might not be the most exciting cars, but they're easy to fix. I'm going to have this baby back up and ready to go in a couple of hours."

"What happened to it?"

"Lost a fight with a rock in the road that was bigger than the owner expected," Olivia said, grabbing a rag off the wheeled cart nearby and wiping the grease and oil from her hands. "But it's nothing I can't handle. Listen, thanks for coming by, because I do have a situation I can't handle, and I wanted to get a read on it from you."

It was then that I noticed the bandage on Olivia's

arm, betraying the cut that had found her in Zoe's emergency room.

"Sure. What's going on?"

"I have another customer who came in the other day. Regular customer, comes in anytime she has a problem with her car. She likes to hang around and chat while I'm working on it, so we've gotten to talking a fair bit. Anyway, when she came in the other day, she had a bruise around her neck. I asked her about it, and she said it was nothing, but she was super evasive about it, you know?"

I nodded. "You think she's being abused?"

"I do. And it's not like there's anything I can do about it, you know? But I thought maybe if you're bored and you feel like doing a good deed…"

"I'm always up for good deeds. What do you know about her?"

"Name is Samantha Groves. She lives in Kihei, not too far from you. She's only lived on the island for about a year. Moved here from California with her boyfriend when her work transferred her to the island. She's some sort of weather researcher for the government. Studies climate patterns, that sort of thing."

"Do you have a name for him? The boyfriend, I mean."

"Sean. That's all I know," Olivia said with a shrug. "I haven't got a last name on him. Anyway, Samantha did me a big favor a couple of months ago. She has a good heart, and I'd hate to see her in an abusive relationship. I don't know. How about if we trade? I'll do some free work on your Jeep for you if you'll look into Samantha and Sean for me."

"Sure," I replied. "I can do that. If he's abusing her, then he should pay for it. I'll consider it my good deed. And if he isn't, and she actually was just in an accident, well, all the better. I'll get some pictures and call the cops if I see anything."

"Thanks, Charlie," Olivia said gratefully. "I appreciate it. I like Samantha, and if she's being abused, I want to do what I can to get her out of that situation."

"Totally. Do you have an address for her?"

"Uh, yeah." Olivia dug out her phone and tapped away for a couple of seconds, then handed it to me. I jotted down the address.

"Do you know anything else about her boyfriend?"

"Only that they've been together for four years. Sean moved here with her. He works in construction."

"And I'm assuming they live together?"

"Sure do. They're both at that address."

"And you said you don't have a last name for Sean?"

"Sorry," Olivia said with a shrug. "I could have asked, but I also didn't want to seem like I was prying, you know? I didn't want her to get suspicious and have her clam up on me completely."

"Sure, I get that. Okay, this should be enough to start with anyway."

"Thanks, Charlie. Consider your next few repairs on the house."

"That sounds great." After all, if the past was

anything to go by, I was going to be making good use of Olivia's services in the future.

"Cool. Thank Zoe again for me, will you? I appreciate her patching me up. Turns out my reflexes aren't quite what they used to be."

"She's pretty great, hey?"

"Totally. If I ever have to go to the ER again, I'm texting you to ask for her schedule so she can patch me up."

I laughed and threw the tennis ball for Egg one last time, said goodbye to Olivia, and headed back home. When it rains, it pours. I now had one more client to look out for. It was time to find out if Samantha was being abused, and if so, to put an end to it.

Chapter 6

I did a slow drive-by of the building complex in which Samantha lived on my way back home. She lived in one of the large complexes right on South Kihei Road that were now used as a mixture of overpriced condos for people actually living on this island and vacation rentals for tourists.

There was a movement gaining increasing popularity on the island to make vacation rentals illegal and to require tourists to stay in accommodations specifically built for them, which would free up much of the residential housing on this island and possibly help make it a little bit more affordable for locals, but so far, the proponents of this plan hadn't had much success. Airbnb and the various vacation rental property management companies still ruled the roost.

Pulling into the complex, I noticed a man on a golf buggy driving slowly through the parking lot. Great. This building had security, like most of the really big complexes on this stretch of road. Mostly, security was there to stop people from poaching a free parking spot from residents, but it was still going to make a stakeout a little bit more annoying.

I parked in a visitor's parking spot near the small office and walked along the road, trying to find the apartment that belonged to Samantha, doing my best to look like a new tourist trying to find their AirBnB. She lived on the second floor, with the living room window facing the parking lot. Perfect. I walked to the building, counted the number of doors, then went back to the lot and made a note of which window was hers. I then went back to my Jeep, leaving without drawing any attention to myself.

I'd come back here tonight and see what I saw. I hoped Samantha wasn't being abused, but if she was, I was going to get proof of it, and put a stop to it.

In the meantime, I figured now was a good opportunity to invest in a top-tier set of binoculars.

I had a pair that I'd temporarily stolen from Zoe, who used them to go bird-watching. But not only would a stronger pair be better for spying on Samantha, I figured I should probably finally buy my own gear, especially as I was regularly getting clients now.

When I got home, my cool new binoculars hanging around my neck, I ran into Franny, my eight-year-old neighbor, waiting for me in the hallway. Her light-brown hair was tied in a ponytail that swung behind her as she ran toward me.

"Cool binoculars," she said excitedly. "Are those the Vortex Diamondback HDs?"

I raised my eyebrows. "Were you waiting for me to come down the hall so you could check them out?"

"Maybe. Was I that obvious? I should have been more subtle." Franny frowned. "I should have brought my swim bag. Something that made it look like I was going out anyway. Or I should have been walking back to the apartment."

"You're a weird kid, Franny, but I like you."

"Thank you. You're a weird adult. Why are you walking around carrying binoculars?"

"Bird-watching."

Franny narrowed her eyes at me. "You are not."

"Am too," I shot back, wondering how *I* was the less mature one in this conversation.

"Fine. What color is the head of a java sparrow?"

"Are you seriously testing me?"

Franny placed her hands on her hips and gave me an impish grin. "Maybe."

"Well, now that I have these binoculars, I can find out. Also, it's red."

"It's black and white."

"Wow, you should tell your dad to take you in for a color-blindness test. It's definitely red."

Franny narrowed her eyes at me. "What are those really for? Are they for spying on people? I bet they are. And can I try them? I've never seen the Diamondback HD before."

I laughed and handed over the binoculars. Franny immediately pressed them against her eyes and swung her head around, looking down the hall. "Wow, these are good!"

"I hope so. They cost a lot."

"Can I borrow them one day?"

"Only if you tell me what for. And how do you recognize these, anyway?"

"I like to do research on all the cool spy stuff I would buy if I was an adult with my own money. All of the websites that review different binocular models list the Diamondback HD as one of the best on the market. Whoever sold you these knew what they were talking about."

"Well, it's good to know I didn't get ripped off."

"I was also looking at them because I want to get a good pair for my birthday. I think it would be fun. I could use them at recess to spy on the other kids and see what they're all up to."

"Maybe when you write your letter to Santa this year, you should ask for a pair," I suggested.

"Do I look like the kind of immature child who still believes in Santa Claus?" Franny asked. "I've known since I was four that it's a story my father invented to hide the fact that all my gifts come from him or from my aunt or my grandparents. I go along with it, because I know he likes to believe I still think a magical man from the North Pole somehow manages to deliver presents in one night to over a billion children worldwide, but the whole thing is ridiculous when you really think about it."

"I should have figured you'd be the kid who doesn't believe in Santa. In that case, maybe if you're lucky, a pair of binoculars will show up under the tree for you this year."

"That would be great! Then I can learn everyone's secrets. Although I'd have to work on my lip reading, first. And maybe I can see dolphins from shore."

"Those both sound like great ideas."

"Okay. I have to go now, before Dad realizes I'm gone and starts to worry. If you ever feel like lending those out, though, I would love to be able to take them to school one day."

"I'll keep that in mind. I do have a client to use these for right now though, but when I'm finished with that case, we'll see."

Franny grinned and waved then spun around on her bare foot and padded back down the hallway the way she had come, disappearing back into her apartment.

I chuckled to myself and entered my own apartment, where Zoe was in the living room, finishing off her book with Coco sleeping on her lap.

"What did Olivia want?" Zoe asked when I entered, shifting to face me while being careful not to disturb the snoring dog.

"She has a case for me. She suspects one of her clients is being abused, and she wants proof before she does anything else."

"Oh, no."

"Yeah. So I'm thinking I might stake the place out tonight, although I'm not a hundred percent sure how I'm going to get to sit in the car, since her complex has security. I checked it out a bit before coming back here. Also, I bought binoculars, but I totally forgot to get food."

Zoe chuckled. "We'll live."

"I know there's pizza dough in the fridge, so I'll make a flatbread for us."

"That sounds great."

I caught Zoe up with everything that had happened while I worked on the dough, topping it with pesto and a bunch of random vegetables I found in the fridge, along with some cheese, and then popping the flatbread into the oven.

"Can I check out the new binoculars?" Zoe asked eagerly, and I handed them to her, plopping myself down on the other end of the couch.

"You sound like Franny. Only if you borrow them, it'll be to *actually* look at Java sparrows or something instead of spying on other people."

Zoe chuckled. "She's a funny kid. I like her though."

"Me too. Anyway, after we eat, I think I'm going to have a nap before my stakeout tonight. I'm working at Aloha tomorrow too. Luckily, not until ten, because I have to meet Heather at six here in town."

"Good call."

At eight o'clock that night, I figured it was time to get going. I still hadn't solved the problem of how I was going to manage the stakeout without security catching me in the act, but whatever. I could wing it.

As I left the apartment, though, and spotted Jake

Llewelyn in the hall, I was hit with a flash of inspiration.

"Hey. How would you like to let me borrow your police badge?" I asked, leaning against the wall next to his door with a grin.

He raised his eyebrows. Tall, with tousled dark hair and smoldering eyes, Jake would have been really hot if he wasn't so infuriating. Okay, he was still really hot. His toned body bulged against his fitted polo, while his fitted navy-blue knee-length shorts revealed that he didn't skip leg day.

"You must have realized before asking that I was going to say no to that."

"It was worth a shot."

"It really wasn't."

"Okay, fine. Do you want to come on a stakeout with me?"

"Are you asking me out on a date?"

"If sitting in a car for hours with somebody to spy on a random couple who might be involved in criminal activity is your idea of a date, I'm starting to understand why you're single."

Jake laughed. "All right, maybe I should have phrased that better."

"You haven't answered me. Are you coming? I was planning on ordering pizza if it takes too long. And I went down to the corner store earlier and got snacks. And Red Bull. So I'm well supplied."

"With that kind of bribe, how can I say no? Who are you staking out, anyway?"

"A friend of mine is worried about one of her

clients and thinks she might be in an abusive relationship. I'm trying to gather evidence one way or the other so that we can then figure out what the next steps are from there."

"And why do you need my police badge?"

"Because the complex she lives in has security in the parking lot, which happens to be the best location to get a look through her living room windows."

Jake pursed his lips. "How long are you planning on being there?"

"Probably until midnight or so? Whenever they go to bed then maybe wait a bit longer to make sure they're really sleeping."

"Okay, I'll come with you. But only because I legitimately believe you'll steal my badge if I say no. And also because if the client's boyfriend is being abusive, he should be stopped."

I grinned. "I knew I could count on you."

"Yeah, yeah. Just know that I've been promised pizza, and you'd better not bail on me."

"That's not a promise I will ever renege on."

"Then by all means, lead the way."

Chapter 7

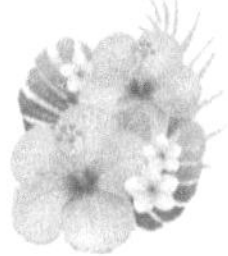

When we reached the parking lot, I was about to get into Queenie, but Jake shook his head.

"You can't seriously expect to do a stakeout in this vehicle."

"What? What's wrong with Queenie? She's great. Besides, I just got the bullet holes fixed."

"The worst part of that last sentence is that I don't even know if you're kidding. Queenie might be a great Jeep, but she stands out like a giraffe trying to blend in with a flock of flamingos. Let's take my car. It's more subtle."

"You drive a Tesla. It's not more subtle."

"Mine is a color that occurs in nature, and it blends in with other cars in a parking lot. Yours is the color of a sign advertising half-price drinks during happy hour. But all right, we can take yours if you insist. Mostly because I don't trust that you aren't going to spill your snacks, and I just had my car detailed a few weeks ago."

"Good. Queenie can be subtle," I said, patting my Jeep. I climbed into the driver's seat then reached into the back, grabbing the big bag of candy, soda, Red Bull, and more and handing it to Jake. "Enjoy. I figure this should get us through the first part of this stakeout."

Jake laughed. "You're much better equipped for this than, well, any cop I've ever met. For us, stakeouts are about bad coffee and hoping you don't have to pee for hours on end."

"That's because cops don't know how to have any fun," I retorted.

"Is that so? You think I can't have fun?"

"You're spending your Friday night sitting in a car with me, spying on a couple people we don't know to see if they're committing a crime."

"That wasn't what I was going to do though. I'm only doing it to be a good person."

"All right, fine. What were your plans before that? A concert on the other side of the island? Bonfire on the beach? Drinking beer with your buddies?"

"If you must know, I was going to spend the evening with Miss Butters while she watched me play *Gran Turismo*. Not the most exciting Friday night, but then again, Miss Butters doesn't talk back as much as you do. I was just stepping out to get some beer, first."

I raised an eyebrow. "And who is Miss Butters? She sounds like the world's least threatening dominatrix."

"Well, in a way, you're not wrong. Miss Butters is my cat."

"How on earth have you never mentioned that you have a cat before?"

"You've never asked," Jake replied with a shrug.

"Okay, as soon as we get into place, I need to see a picture," I said, pulling out of the parking lot.

Jake rifled through the bag and came out with a bag of peanut M&Ms. He tore it open and poured a handful of candy into his hand before wiggling the bag in front of me, silently offering me some.

I opened my palm, and he tipped a handful of M&Ms into it. I began munching on a couple as I drove down South Kihei Road, and within a couple of minutes, I pulled into the complex where Samantha Groves lived. I drove Queenie up to the lot at the back of the complex and parked in an empty spot that faced her living room window.

"Second floor, third from the left," I said to Jake as I turned off the car.

"Well, the lights are on, so it looks like someone is home. They haven't put the blinds down either."

"Thank goodness for people who don't know they're being spied on. Now, I was promised a picture of Miss Butters."

He pulled out his phone, swiped to unlock it, then handed it over. On the screen was a gorgeous cat, predominantly orange with flecks of white on her face.

"Awwww, what a sweetie."

"Miss Butters is a rare female orange cat. I found her behind a dumpster when I was investigating a robbery about two years ago. She came right up to me, meowling. Couldn't have been more than a few weeks old. I shared my sandwich with her—well, the meat in it, anyway—and that was that. I didn't have a say in the matter. They say that you don't adopt a cat, that a cat chooses you, and I never understood what they meant until that moment. I picked her up and brought her into the squad car, where she immediately pooped on the seat."

"I like her already."

Jake chuckled. "Liam complained about the smell, even though I cleaned it immediately. After my shift, I did some googling, stopped by the pet store, and next thing I knew, I had a cat."

"Is she your first pet?"

"Yeah. I figured the lifestyle of a cop wasn't very conducive to having a pet, but it turns out cats are pretty low maintenance. Did you know there are YouTube channels these days that make dedicated cat videos? If I know I'm going to be working a double or triple shift, and Miss Butters is going to be on her own for a while, I stick one of those on. Which I know sounds ridiculous. I never thought I'd be that guy either. But I saw a meme online from a woman who bought her cat an iPad and a yurt, and at least I haven't done that."

"Yet, by the sounds of how things are going," I said with a chuckle. "Miss Butters sounds nice and spoiled. Kind of like Coco, although she likes to nap during the day when I'm not home."

I reached over and grabbed the bag of goodies and

pulled out a can of yellow Red Bull. I pulled open the top and took a long sip then leaned back and looked at the window. While the lights were on, there hadn't been any movement in Samantha's apartment yet.

"So, give me the lowdown on this case," Jake said, grabbing a can of his own and popping it open. "What's the deal?"

"My client believes Samantha is being abused by her boyfriend, Sean. They moved here from the mainland a year ago when she was transferred here for work. She does something in meteorology, and he works construction. Samantha showed up with a few bruises that she explained away, but my client is suspicious. However, she wants proof that Sean is abusive before she takes this any further, obviously."

Before Jake had a chance to reply, I glanced in the rearview mirror and spotted the golf cart that had been patrolling the grounds earlier pulling up behind us. "And now, this is when your badge is going to come in handy."

Jake glanced in his side mirror to have a look as the security guard stepped out and began walking toward the driver's-side door. There had been a shift change since I'd been here a few hours ago. This security guard was a lot bigger than the previous one in both height and girth. I couldn't make out his features in the dark, but his head was shaved bald, and he had a smile on his face as I rolled the window down.

"Hello there," he greeted us. "What are you fine folks doing here this evening?"

Jake smiled at him and flashed his badge. "Just working an investigation, if that's all right with you."

At the sight of the arrow-shaped gold badge with an eagle on top and a picture of the islands of Maui County, the man's eyes widened. "Of course. Sorry to bother you. Although I do have to ask that you register at the office in the morning once they've reopened if that's all right."

"Sure, we'll do that," I lied.

"Great. Thank you very much. I'll leave you be, and you have a good night, okay?"

"You too," Jake said.

The man turned and slowly meandered back to his golf cart.

When I heard the low whirr of the engine as he drove off to continue his patrols, I rolled the window back up.

"What do you think? That there's abuse happening here or that your client is maybe just a little bit overly enthusiastic?"

"I don't get the impression that Olivia's someone who would freak out unnecessarily. If she thinks there's something here, I'd put money on it that she's right. But we'll see. I think we're both hoping she's just been a bit overly cautious, and that there's nothing going on."

"Oh, look, there's someone at the window."

I pulled out my binoculars to get a closer look. Sure enough, Samantha had just entered the living room. She was built slim and looked to be pretty tall, wearing a pair of navy-blue sweat pants and a pink tank top. Her blonde hair flowed in waves past her shoulders, and with these binoculars, I could just make out the bluish hue of a bruise on her neck. Just as Olivia had said. Samantha was absolutely drop-dead gorgeous. She carried a giant bowl of popcorn next to her and settled onto the couch, grabbing the remote and flicking on the TV.

"Think she's going to watch something good?" I asked Jake.

"With a bowl of popcorn that size, I think Sean's not far behind," he replied.

Sure enough, about thirty seconds later, a man walked into view carrying a couple glasses of red wine. Broad-shouldered, wearing a plain gray T-shirt and shorts, with close-cropped brown hair and a round face, he looked, well, a bit like a stereotypical Russian mobster. He even had a half sleeve of tattoos on his right arm.

Sean—at least, I assumed that was him—carefully handed Samantha a glass of wine then joined her on the couch, placing his glass on the coffee table in front of him and wrapping a burly arm around Samantha's shoulders.

Samantha smiled and leaned into the crook of his arm before opening the Netflix app. She scrolled down the list of options before putting on *The Queen's Gambit.*

"Ooh, she has good taste," I said approvingly.

Jake chuckled. "I agree. And I know we've only been here for a few minutes, but I'm not seeing any red flags."

"Neither am I. The fact that he let her pick the TV show *and* seems to happily be watching a show that's primarily aimed at women is a good sign. But you never know. Did you see the bruise on her neck?"

"I did," Jake said, his mouth a straight line. "Someone did that to her, and statistically, it's most likely Sean."

"Okay, so since it looks like we're going to be here a while, I'm going to order pizza. What do you like as toppings?"

"As long as it's normal, I'm happy," Jake said with a shrug.

"Thoughts on pineapple? After all, it's the most controversial of ingredients."

"And the most delicious. We're on Hawaii. I know, I know, Hawaiian pizza was invented in Canada, but I feel like we should still get to stake a claim on it based on name alone."

"That's fair. I'm glad we're on the same page. I couldn't be friends with somebody who doesn't like pineapple on their pizza."

"At least you draw reasonable lines in the sand about people you're friends with."

"I couldn't agree more."

I ordered us a large pizza to share, along with some cheesy bread, and after about ten minutes, Jake got out of the car, offering to pick it up so he could stretch his legs.

I leaned back in the seat, popping open another Red Bull and sipping it slowly while I watched the TV show along with Sean and Samantha. At least *The Queen's Gambit* was actually good. I'd have been pissed if they put something stupid on. And to make things even better, they were one of those couples who watched TV with subtitles on, no matter what. Perfect. That was me at home too. I liked being able to crunch chips loudly without straining to hear what was being said.

A few minutes later, Jake returned with the pizza, the steam from it quickly fogging up the windshield of the Jeep.

"Maybe this was what Leo and Kate were really doing in the back of that car in the *Titanic*," I joked, grabbing a slice. "I'm starving."

Jake laughed. "Yes, I'm sure this is exactly what James Cameron wanted to convey."

He grabbed a piece of pizza himself, and the two of us settled in for a long night of Netflix and stakeout.

"So, what's up with you? I feel like I've barely seen you since the whole thing with Marion Hennessey went down."

I forced a smile. "Oh, you know. Been busy catching bad guys. The usual."

It wasn't entirely a lie. But it wasn't entirely truthful, either. I hadn't been *avoiding* Jake. Okay, maybe one time I came out of my apartment and saw him facing his door and snuck back inside for an extra five minutes to make sure I wouldn't have to talk to him.

The truth was that ever since Rowan McLeod had told me he wouldn't date me while I pined for Jake, I was scared. And I was Charlotte Gibson. I wasn't scared of anything, damn it. So I handled it the way I handled most of my problems: denial and avoidance.

I couldn't say it had been super successful so far, but hey, fiftieth time's the charm, right?

Jake shook his head. "Well, on the bright side, there haven't been that many murders on the island the last few months for you to involve yourself with. Until yesterday, anyway. Did you hear about the one up at Ka'anapali?"

"I did. And let me guess, this is you trying to figure out if I'm working it?"

"You know me too well. But I worry about you."

"You shouldn't. Most of my jobs are spent like this, eating pizza from a box while I spy on people who don't know they're being spied on. And for the record, no, I don't know anything about the case up the coast. But I'm guessing you're not on it either, since it's outside of the Kihei station's purview."

"That's right. Although even if it was my jurisdiction, I wouldn't be working it anyway. Word is the feds have taken over."

I raised an eyebrow. "That's kind of weird, isn't it?"

"Sure is. I've never seen it happen on the island before."

"What's the guy involved with, then? Some sort of mafia stuff? If he was up in Ka'anapali, that would imply he's probably a tourist, right?"

"He was, yeah. I don't know what he was involved in. From what I heard, he was just your regular rich old guy on vacation. But obviously the feds know something we don't, because they don't barge in here and take our cases when they don't have good reason to."

"You're ruining the local-cop-hates-the-FBI trope that television has led me to believe is universal," I said, shooting Jake a sideways glance.

He scoffed as he grabbed another slice of pizza. "That's because it wasn't my case. If that body had dropped in Kihei and I'd been taken off it, I'd be cursing them too. But since it's not, I don't care, and the feds can have it. It might end up being a complicated case too. If the feds are involved, they obviously think it's more than just a run-of-the-mill robbery gone wrong."

"Sounds like it. What do you know about the guy?"

Jake narrowed his eyes. "Are you asking out of curiosity, or…?"

"I'm asking because we're stuck in this car with nothing to do but make conversation. I've already told you, I'm not involved in this."

"Yeah, but you're also the type of woman who would lie to my face to get information from me if you thought it would help you."

Okay, he wasn't wrong. In fact, it was exactly what I was doing.

"That's fair. But I'm telling you, I'm not doing it now."

"It's a moot point, anyway. I don't know anything about the case beyond a bit of chatter I heard at the office. So, how's Coco doing?"

"Oh, you know. Loving the beach, as always. She loves Hawaii. She seems to have more energy here. But then, so do I."

"So you're not going back to Seattle?"

Was it my imagination, or did I detect just the slightest tinge of hope in Jake's voice?

"No. I don't have any plans to anymore. And it's

not just because I like having all my fingers attached to my body. I've started rebuilding my life here. I have a support network. I have a real career. And the more time goes by, the more I realize I'm happy here. I'm content. Maui is my home."

"The islands have a way of drawing you back, don't they?" Jake said. "When I was in the Navy, I was stationed in California for a few months. I thought I'd like it, since I figured the weather would be similar and it would be a lot like being home, but there was nothing quite like the weight lifting from my chest when stepped off that plane again in Hawaii."

I nodded. "I know exactly how you feel. Did you go anywhere cool when you were in the Navy?"

Jake grinned. "Can't tell you. Classified. But yes."

"Well, that's a code for 'no' if I've ever heard one."

"It is not," Jake protested. "It's code for 'that's classified,' so I can't tell you either way."

"I don't believe you," I replied, sticking my tongue out at him. "If you did something awesome, you'd totally tell me, classified or not."

"Oh, yeah? And why would I do that?"

"Because you literally agreed to spend your Friday night sitting in a Jeep that has no lumbar support and spying on a couple just because I wanted access to your badge."

"Well, maybe I just wanted to make sure you didn't get into any trouble."

"I can take care of myself, you know."

"I do know that. But that doesn't make me wrong

either. Marion Hennessey tried to kill you just a few months ago."

"She failed though. Where did you go?"

"Classified."

"You wouldn't have been important enough to go anywhere classified," I teased.

"Oh, I was so important in the Navy," Jake replied with a smirk, and I was pretty sure he was just teasing me back. He lowered his voice. "I've been to places you haven't even heard of."

"Try me," I replied, my voice dropping an octave as well. It felt like the temperature in the car had just gone up ten degrees. I moved closer to Jake, my face only inches from his. "I'm very good at geography."

That was a lie and also the least sexy thing I could have possibly said at that moment, but I wasn't very good at this. It didn't matter. The next thing I knew, Jake's lips locked with mine. My eyes widened in surprise, as if we hadn't been skirting the edge of this particular cliff for ages before falling over it. But I quickly closed my eyes as adrenaline coursed through my veins, the hairs on my arms rising as I ran my hands through Jake's hair. His hands slid down the side of my rib cage, finding my waist and hoisting me out of the driver's seat and onto his lap.

Jake's fingers found the hem of my shirt and pulled it up over my head while mine fumbled with the buttons of his. My hands roamed across his chest even as I pressed my body into his. Our bodies moved together, quickly, with purpose.

There was nothing slow or composed about what

we were doing. We clawed at each other like animals, the line between lust and aggression blurring. Jake clutched at my hair by my scalp and pulled my head back, leaning in and kissing my neck. I pressed my breasts against his chest, feeling it rise and fall with his heavy breaths. My bra came off at one point, and I fumbled with the zipper of Jake's pants.

And that was when there came a rap at the window.

I let out a squeal and grabbed the first thing I could —the empty pizza box—to cover myself, looking over at the security guard who was scowling at us.

"I don't care if you're a cop, this isn't a Motel 6. Get out of here," he said through the window.

"We will. Sorry," Jake replied.

The security guard shot us one last glare before turning around and heading back to his golf cart.

Mortified, I basically dove back into the driver's side of the car. I dug around until I found my shirt and threw it back on while Jake refastened the buttons on his.

I glanced back up at Samantha's window. The lights had gone out. Obviously, she and Sean had gone to bed. There was nothing more we could do here anyway. Throwing the car into reverse, I pulled out of the spot and gunned it back onto South Kihei Road.

We drove in a silence as heavy as our breathing had been only a few minutes earlier. I didn't dare break it. I didn't trust my voice. I was sure my face was the same color as an overripe tomato, and a lump had catapulted itself from its stomach into my throat and lodged there.

I was mortified.

This was *Jake*. Annoying, infuriating, intoxicating Jake.

Wait, why had I said intoxicating?

Even now, I could feel the electricity from his body as he sat in the passenger seat. What was he thinking? Probably the same thing I was.

When we finally reached our apartment building, I pulled into my parking spot and cut Queenie's engine. One of us was going to have to say something. We couldn't just ignore each other forever. I mean, I supposed we could, but eventually, people were going to ask questions.

"So," I started. "How about we pretend nothing happened?" Denial was always my go-to whenever I felt something I didn't want to have to deal with.

"Uh, yeah," Jake said, clearing his throat slightly. "Yeah, that works for me. We made a mistake, and we can just move on from that. It doesn't have to affect anything else."

"Deal. Thanks for coming out with me tonight on a completely uneventful stakeout."

"Anytime," Jake replied.

We walked together in silence until we reached Jake's door. He entered his apartment, and I continued on to mine. I desperately needed a cold shower.

I entered to find Zoe awake, in the kitchen, spreading peanut butter and a sliced banana on a bagel.

Chapter 8

"Hey, Charlie," she greeted me with a smile when I entered. "How was your… wait, weren't you going to go on a stakeout?"

"I was," I replied a little too quickly. "That's where I was. Watching Samantha and Sean watch *The Queen's Gambit*. It was pretty boring, really. Nothing of note worth mentioning at all."

Zoe placed a hand on her hip and looked me up and down, a disbelieving expression on her face. "Really? That's really what you were doing? Because you have a hickey on your neck, and you're not wearing a bra. Oh, and your shirt's on backwards."

"Shit," I muttered, looking down at myself. I was a mess. I really did look like I'd just come back from doing the walk of shame. And boy, was there anything more shameful than having made out with *Jake* of all people?

Zoe chuckled then, bursting my shame bubble.

"Oh, come on, Charlie. You're a grown woman. So you're going to get laid sometimes. It happens."

"Things didn't even get that far," I said, throwing my hands in the air. I didn't even know what I was feeling right now. It was as if my stomach was full of balloons, each one a different feeling, and they'd all been hit with the same dart.

"Then why are you so worked up about it?" Zoe asked, her voice changing to one of concern. "Is everything okay?"

"No, everything is not okay." I could hear the shrillness myself and feel the tightness of my vocal cords. Then I spat it out. "Zoe, I made out with Jake, okay? We were on a stakeout, and we were supposed to be watching Samantha and Sean, and instead, I ended up straddling his lap and undoing his jeans while he pulled off my bra and gave me a hickey. And if it hadn't been for the security guard showing up and interrupting us, we would have gone all the way."

Zoe's mouth opened and then closed. She was speechless.

"So yeah, Zoe, it's embarrassing. It was *Jake*. I have never been this mortified in my life. And I once had sex with a guy who insisted I wear a giraffe onesie while we were doing it."

"What? How did that even work?"

"He cut a hole in the appropriate spot," I replied.

Zoe burst out laughing. Once she started, she couldn't stop. She grabbed at the kitchen counter as tears streamed down her face. "I'm sorry. I'm sorry. It's not funny. Okay, it's not funny to you. But that is hilarious. I can't believe you went along with it."

"Okay, that one's a little bit funny, but this one's not. It was Jake, Zoe. Jake! How am I ever going to live this down?"

"Well, for one thing, Jake is a normal human being who didn't ask you to put a onesie on before you had sex. So he's got that going for him."

"That bar is so low it's just lying on the floor."

"And yet that's apparently all a guy has to climb over. But look, this isn't the end of the world. I know you and Jake have a… tumultuous relationship. I know that better than anyone. The thing is, you're obviously attracted to each other."

"We are not," I shot back.

Zoe raised a single eyebrow skyward and pointedly dropped her gaze to my neck. "As I was saying, you're both obviously attracted to each other. I knew this was going to happen eventually. And I figured you were probably going to freak out about it. So now that it's done, and now that you are, you have to decide what you want to do."

"I'm going to go shower in some bleach and then get a lobotomy, because something is obviously very wrong with my brain."

"Okay, what about after that?"

"I was thinking I might crawl into a corner and just die of shame."

"Okay. You do that, and when I get back from work, maybe your ghost can tell me what the actual plan is here. Because you're going to have to interact with him again in the future."

I groaned and covered my ears. "Can't I just pretend none of this happened?"

"Yes. That is actually one of your options. It's probably not the *best* one though."

"What's my best option?"

"Talk to Jake."

"Nope, I'm going to stop you right there. That's not possible. I'm going to move."

"Back to Seattle?" Zoe asked, raising an eyebrow. "You do realize there are gangsters there who want you dead."

"I would literally rather they chop off all my fingers than have to talk to Jake again. But you're right, Seattle is out. Maybe Phoenix. There's a lot of sun there, right? And no ocean full of sharks. I can hang out with all the old people that have retired there. Maybe I'll learn to play bridge. I can run a private investigation unit out of an old people's home. Help Mabel figure out who stole the last rice pudding from the communal fridge."

Zoe laughed. "Don't let Dot and Rosie hear you talking like that."

"That's a very good point. Anyway, I can't face him. I don't know what I'd say. And we decided we're not talking about it, anyway. We're pretending nothing happened, and we're just going to go on like everything is normal."

"Yes, because that always works so well. Why don't you start by having a shower and sleeping on it? You'll feel better after you get some rest, and maybe you'll stop saying crazy things like you're going to move to Arizona because that's easier than confronting your feelings. And by the way, *this* is why I say you need therapy."

"I actually agree with you for once. I do need therapy. There's obviously something really wrong with me. Zoe, I made out with *Jake*."

"So you've said," she replied, a small smile flickering in the corner of her mouth.

"You're way too calm about this, by the way."

"I'm an emergency room doctor. It's my job to be calm, and besides, this isn't even close to an emergency."

"It is to me," I grumbled.

"I do understand that. And it's going to be okay. I promise. Come on, go to bed."

I glanced over at the clock and frowned slightly. "I can't. I have to meet my new client for coffee at six. And it's already almost one o'clock. The one who's almost certainly an ex-Russian spy, like Rosie. Only I can't let her know about Rosie and her past. I'm too wired to sleep. How can I close my eyes when I know exactly what I'm going to think about?"

"Don't get in over your head, Charlie," Zoe said, her face etched with concern. "I know you're good at what you do, but these are dangerous people."

"I know," I said quietly. "But I have to do it. It's Rosie. She would do the same for me."

"Yes, but the difference is that Rosie is a trained Soviet assassin."

"That's a good point. I will be careful, but I'm going to do this."

"You can't do this if you run away to Phoenix," Zoe pointed out.

I groaned. "Why do you have to make so much sense all the time? Don't you have some lives to save at the hospital or something?"

"I do. I'm leaving soon. Do you want me to drop you off somewhere?"

"No, thanks. I'm going to go have my shame shower and then see my new client. What is wrong with me, Zoe? It's *Jake*."

"Look, I know the two of you have an antagonistic relationship, but on the list of guys you've gotten with, he's actually near the top of the list. He's a normal guy with a steady job and no weird hang-ups. Plus, everyone knows the two of you were bound to get together. It was just a question of when."

I gaped at my best friend. "You did not!"

Zoe shrugged. "You two are the only ones who didn't know."

I rubbed my face. "I can't stand him, and he can't stand me."

"Yes, that's totally why the first time the two of you found yourselves alone in a car in the middle of the night, you came this close to having sex."

I scrunched up my face. "I don't know what's wrong with me."

"Nothing. Nothing is wrong with you. You're a normal woman who happens to be attracted to another normal man. Now, go have a shower, stop it with this crazy talk about moving to Phoenix, and deal with your feelings like an adult instead of running away from them, screaming."

"You can't stop me from overreacting," I said as I shuffled backward, still facing Zoe but moving toward the bathroom.

When I'd closed the door behind me, I leaned against it, pressed my head back against the wood, and sighed. What had I done? Life had been so much easier two hours ago. Zoe was right. I couldn't run away from my problems forever. Besides, I didn't want to live in Phoenix. It got way too hot there in the summer.

I hopped into the shower, letting the hot water flow over my skin and wash away all the emotions of the night. I stared at the water as it flowed down the drain. I wasn't exactly a stranger to bad life decisions, but this one felt like one of the worst I'd ever made.

Jake? Of all people, Jake? Really? What was wrong with me?

I mean, he is pretty hot, a tiny voice in the corner of my brain argued, but I pushed it back. It didn't matter how hot Jake was. He was infuriating. Annoying. All kinds of adjectives.

I ran my fingers through my hair as I leaned my head back and was instantly reminded of the feeling of Jake doing the same.

Ugh.

I had to stop this. I reached over to the shower handle and slammed it to the right, and the hot water falling over me instantly turned to ice. I let out a gasp as my insides twisted and clenched at the sensation for a few seconds until my body accustomed itself to the feeling of the cold water. After about ten seconds, I turned off the shower and climbed out, grabbed my towel from the rack on the wall, and wrapped it around me.

Everything was going to be okay. Zoe was right. This wasn't the end of the world. It was one little mistake.

But why did that mistake have to feel so good?

Chapter 9

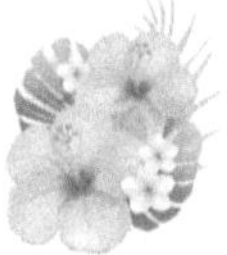

By the time I got back to the kitchen, Zoe had a cup of coffee waiting for me, which I gratefully inhaled. I was going to be running on caffeine and fumes today, no doubt about it.

"Feeling better?" she asked as she loaded up her purse, getting ready for work.

"I guess," I said, throwing my head back. "I'll live."

"Well, that's good to know. That's step one."

"Why did it have to be *him*?"

"I'll let you sit with that one for a while on your own. I have to get to work. You're going to be fine, Charlie."

"I know. But I'm going to be whiny about it first."

"I wouldn't expect anything else. Try and have a good day, okay? And maybe find a therapist to whine to."

"I don't need therapy, I need chocolate. You too. I hope you have good surfing conditions after your shift."

"Thanks," Zoe said with a smile. Then, with a quick wave, she was off.

I leaned back against the couch and sighed. It was going to be a long day.

AROUND A QUARTER TO SIX, I LEFT THE APARTMENT to meet up with Heather. She was already waiting for me at the coffee truck when I arrived. I pulled Queenie over in the large lot and walked over to the main area. About a half dozen food trucks were organized in a rectangle, with ten or so picnic tables in the center area between them all.

At this early hour, with the sun not yet risen above Haleakala to the east, only the Kraken Coffee truck was open. The others were shuttered, sitting still in the darkness of the morning. Heather sat at one of the picnic tables, her back to one of the closed trucks, facing the gap in the vehicles that served as an entrance. I recognized that move immediately; Rosie did exactly the same thing. She always sat with her back to a wall, facing the door, and whenever she entered a room, if I watched carefully, I could see her looking around for the exits.

Once a spy, always a spy, I guess.

Dressed in a floral-print top and shorts that reached just above her knee, with a straw hat on her head, Heather was the picture of elegance this morning. She nodded when she spotted me. I placed my order at the counter and joined her with a triple-shot latte a couple minutes later, the weathered wood creaking slightly under my weight as I sat down.

Beneath one of the trailers to the right came a bit of a scuffle; the chickens that lived in the lot were waking up. It wouldn't be long before the roosters decided to announce the sun's arrival.

"Good morning," I said to Heather.

"Thank you for meeting me. You're willing to take my case? I need to know who killed my husband."

"I am," I said slowly. "But I have conditions. First of all, you can't mention my friends to anybody. This is my case and my case alone. They cannot be involved."

"Understood. Believe me, I know what is at stake." Heather's mouth was a firm line. She was all business.

I gave a curt nod, matching her energy. "Good. Secondly, I need to know *everything*. I know secrets is what you traded in, but you can't keep them from me. Not if you want your husband's killer to be found. Not if you want to know if whoever killed him is after you too. I'm not going to go tattling on you to the CIA. But I can't try and solve two mysteries at once."

"I will not lie to you, either directly or by omission. My husband is dead, and there is nothing I can do to change that, but I need to know that my family and I are safe, and I will do whatever it takes to ensure that."

"Okay, good. We have an agreement."

"Yes. Now, what do you need to know?"

"Tell me everything, from the beginning."

Before Heather could reply, a rooster near the Kraken Coffee truck lifted his head and did a loud cock-a-doodle-doo, announcing the start of a new day.

When he was finished, Heather looked at me. "Rex and I were assigned to be husband and wife when we landed in America. We had different identities then, of course. Your friend—she's not CIA, is she?"

"I'm not at liberty to say," I replied, doing my best to keep every muscle in my face relaxed. I didn't want to give anything about Rosie away. "We're not here to talk about her. So, you landed at JFK, and you were told to begin a relationship with Rex?"

Heather nodded. "Yes. I was nervous, of course. You never knew what kind of man you'd end up with. We were both in service to Khrushchev, though this was only a few months before Brezhnev took over. I was assigned to live in Annapolis, Maryland."

"The Naval Academy," I said.

Heather nodded. "Yes. Our roles were to infiltrate and gather as much intelligence as we could from the campus. Generally, we targeted off-campus bars students were known to frequent. We were good at our jobs, but it was… well, it was difficult. I didn't enjoy it. I thought I would, but I didn't. And I soon found that Rex felt the same way. He had nearly been caught a couple of times. He could be sloppy, Rex. And aggressive. He always got information, but he wasn't as subtle as he needed to be. More sledgehammer than scalpel. They tried to train it out of him back in Leningrad—sorry, St. Petersburg—but the more time he spent away from them, the more he reverted to his instinctive ways of doing things. Then one day, he got caught. He was too sloppy. He returned home and told me we had to get out, immediately."

"What did you do?" I asked, completely enraptured by her story.

"We couldn't go to our handler. We'd be punished, sent back to Russia, and our professional careers would be over. If not our lives. Spies were a very sensitive business back then. And of course, if we stayed in America, we'd be caught by the CIA, and that wouldn't have a happy ending, either. So, I told Rex our one hope was disappearing. I had ten thousand dollars stashed under a mattress for emergencies. That was a lot of money back then. I took it and bought the two of us tickets for the next train to St. Louis. From there, we travelled to Chicago then Philadelphia and finally to New York City. In the seventies, it was easy to get new, fake identification downtown in Manhattan. Our old lives were dead. We were Rex and Heather Thunder. I wasn't a big fan of the name, but Rex insisted. And we began our new lives."

"And you never once ran into anything suspicious before yesterday?"

"No," Heather replied. "And believe me, I was watching over my shoulder the entire time. Even after the wall came down and the Cold War ended, I wasn't sure we were safe. Memories are long. Longer than political regimes. And now Rex has been murdered, and I don't know who did it. The FBI has taken over this case. They spoke to me yesterday. I don't trust them. Not only do I dislike them on principle, but the two agents they have in charge are idiots. I need someone to get to the bottom of this case for me, for real."

"Okay. Tell me about your lives now and who you know on this island."

Heather took a deep breath, pressing her lips together for a moment, and then continued. "There was Rex and me, of course. And our daughter, Melissa. She's the one getting married. Our two sons are here too. David and John. They're older than Melissa; in their forties. She was a late-in-life surprise, but one I wouldn't have given up for the world. And of course, Melissa's fiancé, Chet. And then there are two hundred and seventy-seven friends and family members on top of that who flew out for the wedding."

My eyes widened. "Two hundred and seventy-seven?" I was pretty sure I didn't even know a hundred and seventy-seven people by name, let alone well enough to invite them to my wedding.

The corner of Heather's mouth curled into an amused smile. "Rex and I made a fortune in real estate, allowing us to give our children the best possible start in life without having our faces plastered all over the newspapers. In fact, we worked diligently to ensure our family's privacy. And Melissa and Chet are both very successful in their own right. Melissa is the editor for one of the largest home décor magazines in the country, and Chet owns a small chain of fitness studios. Between them, they've got quite the social circle."

Heather sat up and straightened her back when she spoke about her daughter, the pride evident in her voice.

"Okay. The thing is, I need to know if any of these people had anything against Rex. Anything that might lead them to want to kill him. Because I can't discount the fact that this might just be an opportunistic crime, a regular murder committed by someone he knows and not an assassination by spies."

Heather swallowed hard. "Yes. I thought you would say that. And believe me, I am not the kind of woman to allow sentiment to cloud my rational judgement. I spent all of yesterday asking myself who in my family's close circle of friends might want to see Rex dead. The fact is, I can't see anyone having a motive to actually *kill* him. Rex was a good man. A kind man. He partially funded Chet to help him start up his company, you know? That's the kind of person he is. But then, people kill over anything, don't they?"

I sat back and let Heather continue. Despite her calm exterior, the way she tapped her fingers nervously against her coffee cup and the way she rambled slightly told me there was more to come.

"But then, Chet's been having trouble paying Rex back. I do know that. Would he kill him over it? I certainly hope not. My daughter is supposed to marry him. And I don't see Chet as being that type, but you never really know, do you? I've met thousands of people over the years who wouldn't think me the type to be a Russian spy, and yet here we are."

"I'll look into Chet discreetly."

"Thank you. For what it's worth, I don't believe someone in our entourage did this."

"Is the wedding still going forward?"

"Yes. I spoke with Melissa yesterday. She's obviously broken up, but she wants to hold it. She knows everyone travelled a long way to come to her wedding, and she thinks Rex would want her to go through with it. She wants to do it as part of her grieving process."

"Right. Can you let me know if any members of the entourage suddenly disappear or if any of your guests decide they have to suddenly go back to the mainland?"

"Of course. But I'm telling you, I don't think it was anybody from our regular lives."

I nodded. "I know. I'm going to investigate every avenue. What about anybody here? Have you noticed anyone following you? Anyone taking a peculiar interest in your family?"

"Nothing of the sort. And believe me, if there was something like that going on, I'd have noticed."

"Can you run me through the events of that morning, when Rex was killed?"

"We woke up early given the jet lag. I was up just after four, and Rex awoke about twenty minutes after I did. He went through his morning routine and then went to his suite to get some work done, as he did every morning."

"Do you know what he was working on, exactly?"

"He told me it was a business deal back in New York. Something about a plot of land in Brooklyn that he thought was prime for redevelopment. But he wasn't sure it was going to go through. There was some sort of hang-up, which was why he was working while in Hawaii."

"Is that normal?"

Heather barked out a humorless laugh. "Goodness,

yes. You show me a smooth real estate deal on that scale and I'll know I've died and gone to heaven. No, it was issue after issue, but it always is. The deals don't always go through, but that's business. He was on the phone with some people and then on the computer, and eventually Rex emerged and told me he was going out before breakfast. He wanted to clear his head a little."

"Did you think this was out of the ordinary at all?"

"Oh, no. Rex enjoyed walking to solve his problems. He would regularly go out late at night when we lived in New York, when it was dark. He thought it was the best way to organize his thoughts and think his way through a problem."

"You didn't worry about him?"

"No more than I worried at any other time. It wasn't street thugs or opportunistic muggers that were on my mind. And the spy agencies wouldn't wait until nighttime to act; a brazen daytime kidnapping was just fine to them. But this time, he didn't come home. I started to worry after about an hour, and then there was a knock on the door, and I got the news."

"All right. I think that's all the questions I've got for now."

"Thank you, Charlie." Heather paused. "Look, I know Rex. I know my husband. He was older, of course, but he wasn't frail. He wasn't weak, and he wouldn't have let his guard down. I don't think this was an ordinary murder. This is the key that will get you into our hotel room. The old one. Room 1015. Don't tell anyone where you got it, obviously. But if he had something, it would have been hidden. I wouldn't have looked for it. I wasn't that kind of wife. Now, I have to go. Nobody knows I'm meeting you, and I have to be back at the hotel to meet my daughter shortly. The rehearsal dinner is tonight, and I've got a funeral to organize as well."

"I'm very sorry for your loss. Thanks for the key. Just quickly: where would a former Soviet spy hide something in a hotel room?"

Heather smiled. "Somewhere well hidden. I'm afraid I don't know more than that. I… mentally, I wanted to disconnect from my old life completely. I've been looking over my shoulder for decades, but at the same time, if there were any clues that my husband was up to something, I ignored them. I'm sorry I can't be more helpful. I don't know what you think of us, but for all his faults, Rex was a good man. I just hope you won't be finding my body anytime soon. Or my family's."

Heather swallowed hard, and I realized then just how scared she really was for her children. There were a lot of lives at stake here. It wasn't just about making sure Rosie's secret was safe. I had to solve this case, and fast.

Chapter 10

I left Heather with a lot to chew on. Since I was in the area, I drove by Samantha Groves's apartment just to see if there was anything going on there, but all the lights were off, and there was no sign of life.

I pulled out of the parking lot quickly, not wanting to be seen by the security guard, my face still flaming as I remembered what I had done with Jake. I did my best to squash all those feelings as far down as I could. Then I headed over to Dot's place to catch her and Rosie up on my conversation with Heather before I had to be at Aloha Ice Cream for my shift starting at ten.

Dot opened the door when I knocked and looked me up and down. "Pulled an all-nighter, did you?"

"Is it that obvious?" I asked, stifling a yawn.

"You can have a quick nap on the couch if you'd like. Rosie's going to be here in about an hour."

"I wanted to let you know what I learned from Heather," I said, recounting the whole story.

Dot frowned. “No obvious suspects then. Other than Chet. But why would he wait until a couple days before his wedding to murder his future father-in-law? Surely he could get away with it in New York.”

“That’s what I’m going to find out,” I said. “Do you mind looking into Chet while I try and get a bit of shut-eye?”

“Sure, no problem,” Dot said.

I collapsed on her couch, and if she said anything else, I didn’t hear it. I must have been asleep within seconds. So much for the three shots of caffeine I’d just inhaled.

When I woke up, to the sound of the front door opening, I felt vaguely human again. It was amazing how even an hour’s sleep could completely change the way I felt.

Rosie entered, carrying a four-pack of Red Bull, which she waved in my direction. “I was told this might come in handy for you.”

“You’re a lifesaver,” I said. I cracked one open and guzzled the candy-like liquid.

“Charlie met with Heather,” Dot explained and summarized the meeting we’d had.

“So she is worried,” Rosie said, pressing her lips together. “Heather doesn’t believe it was someone in her close circle. Frankly, the fact that the FBI has been brought in makes me think she may be correct. Certainly, someone has realized this isn’t a run-of-the-mill case. If you ask me, the CIA knew who Rex really was. Because they can’t be seen acting on American soil, they've called in the FBI to take care of the investigation on the ground."

"I'm going to go by the hotel today after my shift and see what I can find out. Dot, did you get anything on Chet, the fiancé?"

Dot nodded. "Oh, so much. He's a total gym bro. The kind of man who lives at the gym, whose diet consists mainly of protein shakes and boiled chicken and who won't stop talking about his macros."

"Or his PB on bench?" I asked with a smile.

"Exactly. I dug into his history a little bit. It seems he's lifting bigger numbers on the bar than on the balance sheet. Basically, Chet's business is on the verge of bankruptcy. He owns seven different gyms in New York City. The company is called—get this—TestosterZone."

I scrunched up my nose. "I can already smell the B.O. So it's not going well?"

"No. And you have to watch this video I found on his website, because I had to see it, and I feel like the two of you should suffer too."

Dot tapped at her mouse a couple of times, and a YouTube video opened on the main monitor.

The video started with a montage of typical power-lifting gym footage: a pair of hands adding a forty-five-pound plate to a bar, a man grimacing as he did a bench press, a single trickle of sweat dripping down his brow, a guy doing bicep curls with a dumbbell that looked like it weighed as much as I did. Then the camera cut away to a shot of a man guzzling down a protein shake, his Adam's apple bobbing up and down as he swallowed, looking weirdly erotic.

Then the video cut to footage of the gym floor. In the background, men were pumping iron, grunting away as they lifted weights. In the foreground stood a man in a tank top with TestosterZone emblazoned across the front in a font that evoked the mid-nineties. He was certainly fit but without being *so* muscular that he'd place in an Arnold Schwarzenegger lookalike competition. Still, he was lathered up with more oil than the coast of Alaska after the Exxon Valdez disaster. He was pretty good-looking, with dark hair gelled back, deep-set black eyes, and a couple days' worth of stubble across his strong jaw.

Across the bottom of the screen, the words "Chet Struckman—Owner" flashed in a font that matched the company's logo.

"Hi, I'm Chet, owner of TestosterZone," Chet said. "If you're tired of working out at gyms that make you feel bad for wanting sick gains, then this is the place for you. Here at TestosterZone, we're all about crushing goals, whatever they may be. You're not going to get in trouble for putting too much weight on the bar here or get stares when you grab the big dumbbells. After all, no curls, no girls, right?" He chuckled at his own joke.

My expression turned to one of disgust. "Wait, this is supposed to *promote* the company?"

"We have seven convenient locations around the New York area, with flexible hours to accommodate your busy schedule."

At that second, a guy dressed like he was getting ready for his latest WWE fight walked past the camera.

"Hey, keep it real, Gainzilla," the man said, fist bumping Chet as he walked past.

"You too, brother," Chet called out after him. "You see? Here at TestosterZone, we're all about a supportive atmosphere. Bros supporting other bros. And we aren't sexist or anything. Ladies can be bros too. In fact, we have over five female members now. So if you're looking for a place that won't shame you for trying to work out like a real man, where creatine isn't a bad word, and where the trainers actually know the difference between Romanian and sumo deadlifts, this is the place. Come, join us. Become a TestosterBro, and come build yourself a better body. Because no one ever built muscle riding a boring elliptical."

Chet thumped his chest with a closed fist a couple of times and jutted his chin out at the camera before the screen faded to black. The company logo appeared at the top, followed by addresses for all seven gyms.

"Wow," I finally said. "Five entire women between all seven locations. He must be so proud. I'm just glad he only used the word 'female' once. Honestly, the most disappointing part of that video is that the guy who owns this company somehow has been able to open seven locations."

Dot snorted. "But the thing is, I dug into the numbers. He's expanding too quickly. If he'd just focused on his first location, on Staten Island, he would probably be fine. He might even be pulling in a profit.

But he decided to go for massive growth right off the bat, and as a result, he's deep in the red."

"That makes sense given as he's having trouble paying Rex back. Okay, I'll look into him further."

"I think that's smart. Money makes people kill. You never know; it's possible Chet wanted to get out from under that loan and figured killing Rex was the best way to do it."

Rosie's lips were pursed, and she tilted her head slightly to the side.

"You don't think he did it," I said to her, more statement than question.

"I wouldn't rule anything out at this point, obviously. But I think it's unlikely. It would be like someone getting a jump on me. Sure, it's possible. But can you really imagine it happening?"

"No," I admitted.

"That said, if he has a motive, I'd certainly look into him. I also wouldn't write him off as some kind of mole. After all, what if he got involved with the daughter, Melissa, to get closer to Rex?"

"Also a good point. After work today, I'm going to drive up there and see what I can find out. Heather gave me a key to her old hotel room, and I'd like to get in there and have a look. I'm just at the information-gathering stage right now."

"I'll see what I can find out about Rex without setting off any alarm bells," Dot said. "It'll be good to know exactly what we're dealing with."

"And you're staying out of this," I said to Rosie. "I know it goes against every instinct you have, but right now, you really do need to lie low. Let Dot and me take care of this. It's already bad enough that there's going to be one degree of separation between you and this investigation, but let's not make it zero. You're supposed to be a retired bank teller pottering along, not investigating a murder."

"All right, all right," Rosie said, but I could tell she wasn't pleased about it despite knowing I was right.

"I'll let you know what I find out tomorrow, okay?"

After a long shift at Aloha Ice Cream, made slightly less hellish thanks to a lunch that consisted of an espresso milkshake and two more Red Bulls—I briefly wondered if there was a daily limit on how many you were supposed to drink—I drove Queenie up to Ka'anapali. I lucked into a free spot as someone pulled out of the nearby lots. I threw on a wig I'd bought exactly for situations like this, a big pair of sunglasses that hid half my face, and a giant sunhat to complete my disguise. Armed with the keycard to Heather and Rex's room, I made my way to the Beach Dreams Resort Maui, one of the most luxurious hotels on this part of the island.

Located next to the Sheraton, Beach Dreams was a ten-story-high building overlooking the water. I walked toward the entrance, where the bellboys in Hawaiian shirts and cargo shorts nodded a hello, which I returned. Hawaiian music strummed over the loud-speakers, still audible over the sound of the dramatic waterfall set up in the entrance, the cascade tumbling from the second floor into the enormous fountain in the lobby.

The lobby level essentially spanned the first two stories and was open all the way through to the beach on the other side. To my left was a bank of elevators, and I pressed the button to go up. It required the rider to tap their keycard before allowing access to the floor they wanted, and I made note of that. Had Rex's killer had to wait for him to be outside because they weren't able to get to the tenth floor?

The doors opened to a standard hotel hallway. The walls were white and airy, the carpet underfoot cyan. Bright lighting filled the hall as I followed the signs to get to the room, but when I reached it, not only was there yellow tape across the door, but a seal emblazoned with the FBI's logo made it impossible to enter the room without the intrusion being noticed.

Damn.

I continued along the hall without stopping. About three doors further along, I stopped, reached into my bag, pretending to look for my key. When I couldn't find it, I headed back to the elevators, scouring the floor the entire time, as if I'd lost it somewhere nearby.

When I was back in the lobby, I called Dot. "I need you to hack into the Beach Dreams security camera footage for me," I said when she answered.

"You always know what to say to a woman to make her smile," Dot replied. "I'll do my best. If they're on an internal network, I might not be able to access it though."

"I have faith in you."

"So you should. But if it's on an internal network and I don't get anything back when I ping it, I'll need physical access to the hub controlling it. And that's not impossible to do, but it'll take longer."

"Can you call me back when you know if the internal networking and pinging and hubs worked?" I asked.

Dot chuckled on the other end of the line. "Your generation is supposed to be great with computers. You grew up with them."

"I know how to use Google, and that gets me through ninety percent of what I need a computer for just fine."

"Until you have to call me to hack into hotel security for you. Anyway, don't worry about hanging up. I'm already in. This was child's play. I bet the manager hired their thirteen-year-old niece to do all the security because kids are supposed to be good with computers. So, what do you need from me?"

"I need the footage from elevator one and from the tenth floor for the last five minutes to be erased. And then I need you to loop footage of both being empty again for another ten minutes or so."

"Copy that. Do you need me to come up there and give you a hand?"

"Not unless you were secretly part of a circus growing up. Thanks though."

"All right. Let me know if you need anything else."

"I'll probably text. My phone's going to be on silent

too. Technically, I'm about to break into a crime scene."

"Good luck."

I ended the call and blew out a puff of air as I put the phone back into my pocket. I was going to need it.

Chapter 11

I waited about thirty more seconds and then stepped back into the same elevator, going back up to the tenth floor. I walked past Rex and Heather's old room and knocked on the room one door over. Nothing. So I continued on. At the second door, at the end of the hall, next to the staircase, someone answered.

The occupant was an older woman, probably in her seventies. She wore a cotton shirt in a floral pattern that had probably been stolen from some seventies wallpaper and a pair of oversized cargo shorts. She couldn't have been taller than four foot ten. Her curly white hair surrounded her head like an unruly halo, and her cat's-eye glasses were at least an inch thick, but she still squinted to get a good look at me.

"Hello?" she said in a strong New York accent. "Who are you?"

"Hi. I'm from next door, and this is embarrassing, but I've lost my room key. I left my balcony door open, and I'm wondering if I could just pop over onto yours and head back to my room," I said in as friendly a voice as I could manage. "I'll only be a moment."

The woman squinted at me, looking suspicious. "I don't know. Why don't you just ask reception for another key?"

"I was out by the pool, and I don't have any of my ID on me," I said with what I hoped looked like an embarrassed shrug, wondering if maybe this had been a bad idea. On the bright side, I was pretty sure this lady wouldn't be able to describe me to anyone. She appeared to be blind as a bat. Between that and my disguise, I figured I was good to go.

"You sure this doesn't have anything to do with that dead man a couple doors down? You're not some sort of reporter, are you?"

"No, ma'am, I'm not."

"And how am I supposed to take your word for it?"

"You just have to trust me."

"And what about if I let you in and you rob me? You know, it used to be only men that did that sort of thing, but thanks to feminism, now even women can rob old ladies in their hotel rooms. It never used to be that way, you know? You knew to be wary of men and only men. It's exhausting having to watch out for women too. But at the same time, I suppose if men are getting free cash from robbing unsuspecting tourists, why shouldn't women do the same? You're not going to rob me though, are you?"

"I promise you, I will not."

"Good. Because I might look old, but I'm warning

you, I have a cane, and I know how to use it. Yogi Berra himself came down to my neighborhood one day when I was seven years old, and he taught all us kids how to hit. You know what he said to me?"

"No."

"Yogi Berra said it's all about timing. If you got the timing, it'll go. And I might be older than dirt, young lady, but I got the timing. So if you're about to try any funny business, you better think twice."

I held up my hands in mock surrender. I probably should have just broken the seal and let the feds deal with the fact that someone broke into their crime scene. This lady was nuts, and I was pretty sure she was itching to beat me to a pulp with her cane. "I'm not going to try anything funny. Now, can I please just climb onto your balcony?"

"All right," the lady said, narrowing her eyes in suspicion as she opened the door wide.

I stepped in gingerly, making an effort to stay as far away as I could from the woman's purse, which sat on a side table near the door. The woman followed me, holding her wooden cane like a baseball bat aimed at my head. Great. Everything I'd heard about New Yorkers was true. I immediately headed to the balcony and stepped outside, hoping that would satisfy her and keep my brains from being bashed in by a walking implement.

"Thank you very much," I told her when I was safely outside and she'd lowered the cane, tapping it in her palm as if it was a nightstick.

"You're welcome, dear. Now, no offense, but I'm

going to lock you out there. Take better care of your things next time."

"Will do," I said cheerfully as I heard the click of the lock. I had expected the old lady to turn and go back to what she was doing, but no. She planted her feet firmly in front of the locked door, stuck her hands on her hips, and stared me down.

Cool, that was exactly what I wanted. An audience.

Trying my best to ignore the crazy lady on the other side of the glass, I inspected the task before me. The balconies for each hotel room were separated by about a foot of space, which, in normal circumstances, wouldn't have been far at all. But suddenly, I was ten stories above the concrete below, and ten stories might as well have been ten thousand feet.

I mean, if I fell, the result would be the same. I'd be ground pizza.

I tried not to think about that too much. I headed to the aluminum railing and grabbed it to see how stable it felt. It didn't move under my touch, which was a good sign. I could do this.

Then I made the mistake of looking down. The world suddenly began to swim beneath me. My throat clenched shut faster than a teenager pulling on the strings of his hoodie. Maybe this was a bad idea.

"Hey, lady! Are you going, or are you squatting on my balcony? Come on, I don't have all day," the old lady shouted from behind the glass.

I sighed. I supposed I didn't really have any other options.

I carefully hoisted myself onto the railing and

jumped across to the next balcony over. I landed on the concrete with a thud, falling onto my shoulder, but at least I was on solid ground and not plunging to my death below. One down, one more to go.

With my confidence inflated from my successful first attempt, I launched myself over the second balcony's railing and landed on Rex and Heather's balcony. I actually landed on my feet this time and stabilized myself by grabbing the arm of one of the balcony chairs.

"That's right, I'm basically Catwoman," I muttered to myself as I desperately hoped the balcony door had been left unlocked.

I pulled on the door, but no such luck.

"Why do I not think of these things *before* I start them?" I muttered to myself as I sat on the concrete, staring at the door. I had to call Rosie. She would know what to do.

"Hey!" the old lady suddenly called out.

I jumped about a foot in the air.

"What are you doing?"

"Getting into my room," I shot at her.

"I'm old, not stupid. That's not your room. That's the one where the dead guy and his wife were staying. You are a reporter, aren't you?"

"No," I said quickly. "I'm not. I'm a private investigator, and I'm working for the wife."

"Then why didn't you say that when you knocked on my door?"

"Because I didn't think you'd let me in."

"Damn right I wouldn't. This is a police matter. Let the police deal with it."

"I was literally hired to do this."

"To commit a crime? I don't think so."

"What are you going to do from there, throw your cane at me? Yogi Berra wasn't a pitcher."

The old lady harumphed in my direction. "You know, back in my day, people respected the police."

"I'm respecting them by solving this crime for them. Now, are you just going to stand out here and yell at me, or are you going to let me do my job?"

The old lady muttered something inaudible but turned and went back into her room.

I pulled out my phone and called Rosie.

"Hello?" she answered on the first ring.

"Hi, Rosie. I'm wondering if you can give me a hand with something."

"Given as I've spent the entire day pottering around the garden with the property manager at my place, pretending that I give a crap about the difference between a coral tree and erythrina, I would *love* the opportunity to be helpful."

"In that case, can you tell me how to get into a hotel room if I'm standing on the balcony and staring at a locked patio door?"

Rosie scoffed. "Oh, that's one of the simplest breaking-and-entering situations alive. Believe me, once you know how easy it is to break into a patio door, you'll never look at yours the same way again. I assume you've checked if it's locked?"

"I might not be a super-spy like you, but yes, I have checked. It's locked."

"In that case, the easiest thing to do is to simply lift the door off its hinge. Press yourself against the door, dry your hands on your clothes, and put them on the glass, your fingers spread apart and digging into the glass to get as much purchase as possible. Then stand on your tiptoes. You should be able to get enough purchase to lift the whole door and take it off the tracks. Once you're inside, just lift it back onto the tracks. And don't forget to wipe off your fingerprints."

"Wow, it's really that easy?" I asked.

"It most certainly is. As far as home security goes, patio doors are awful. Now, give it a try. If it doesn't work on the first attempt, try a few more times. If you're really stuck, call me back, and we'll try another way."

"Thanks, Rosie. I appreciate it."

"Not a problem at all."

I ended the call and did as Rosie had described. The first and second attempts failed miserably, but the third time around, I really pressed my fingers against the glass and used my body to hoist the whole door upward. It shifted in the frame, and sure enough, a moment later, it escaped the tracks completely.

I let out a yelp as I just about dropped the entire door in surprise, but at the last second, I was able to grab a firm hold of it. Once I was safely inside the hotel room, I put the door back on the tracks then went back outside and wiped my fingerprints off the glass.

I sent Rosie a quick text letting her know it had worked, slipped on a pair of latex gloves that I'd brought with me, and set about looking for anything that might give me an idea as to who would have wanted Rex dead.

The patio opened onto the open-plan living and dining area of the two-bedroom suite. To my left was a sixty-five-inch, wall-mounted TV. In front of it was a full-sized cream-colored sectional sitting on a plush beige rug. A wooden coffee table split the two.

Behind the couch were a dining table and six chairs and an expansive entry leading to the hall outside.

I peered into the two bedrooms. Each featured a king-sized bed. One had a loveseat on the far end and the other a desk. This was obviously the space Rex had been using as an office, and I decided to start there.

His laptop had been removed by the feds, obviously, and I imagined any notes had too. But I wasn't looking for something obvious; I was looking for what the feds might have missed.

I sat at Rex's desk, trying to imagine what I'd do if I were secretly some sort of spy.

Obviously, I wouldn't keep anything on my normal computer in case it got into the wrong hands. I'd have to hide the information I was keeping somewhere. Probably on a thumb drive. That was how everyone did it in the movies, and while Rosie always complained Hollywood got things wrong, it couldn't be *everything.*

And even if it wasn't a thumb drive, something had to be hidden somewhere.

I ducked underneath the desk and looked at the underside in case Rex had hidden something there.

Then I removed all the drawers from the desk and systematically checked every inch for some sort of hidden panel or secret compartment or even just a bunch of notes taped beneath one of them.

But no, nothing. I sat on the floor, surrounded by drawers of the now-practically-dismantled desk, frowning. That had been my best idea, and it had all come to nothing. Okay, it had also been my only idea.

Where else would a spy hide something important? And of course, I was also assuming that if there *was* something here—not a guarantee—the feds hadn't found it first. What if I was on the wrong track entirely? What if Rex had nothing to do with espionage anymore, and like Heather, he was just trying to live out his golden years without the past catching up to him? What if it was as simple as Chet not wanting to pay back Rex for the money he'd put into the business?

No, something about that theory didn't feel right. Maybe it was what Rosie had said. Someone like Chet would have a really hard time surprising someone like Rex enough to kill him. Or maybe Chet just wasn't finished using Rex as a portable ATM to keep his business afloat.

Something still felt wrong about it, but I had no other options. I left the bedroom being used as an office and explored the rest of the hotel room. To my chagrin, almost everything else had been removed. The feds were nothing if not efficient. Frankly, apart from the black fingerprint powder everywhere and the unmade beds, this suite almost looked like the occupants had checked out and it was ready to go for the next visitor.

I must have spent fifteen minutes scouring every inch of the place, but I came up empty once more. Eventually, I sighed, realizing that I'd probably committed a felony for nothing. I decided to put the desk back together and find a way to get out of here that hopefully didn't involve another interaction with the world's nosiest neighbor. Heading back into the extra room, I frowned when I looked at the wall behind the desk.

There were two sets of power outlets, set about three inches apart. And sure, at first glance, that wasn't the weirdest thing ever. After all, this was a desk, and people tended to need more power for their electronics these days than they used to. But it was still a little out of the ordinary to have that many outlets, and so close together, especially in a hotel room. Then, beneath one of the outlets, on the hardwood floor, was just a little bit of dust that didn't look natural. I ran my finger across the floor and had a closer look. I was pretty sure it was drywall dust.

Something weird was going on here. I quickly put the drawers back into the desk, and my phone began to ring.

"Damn it," I muttered as I pulled it from my pocket and checked the caller ID. It was Heather. I slid my finger across the screen to answer then put her on speaker and laid the phone on the ground as I set about investigating this outlet.

"Hi, Heather."

"Charlie," she said. "Listen, did I see you on the balcony to our old room about twenty minutes ago?"

"Not if you ask me in front of anyone else, but yes."

"In that case, if you're still in the room, you'd probably like to know that the FBI have arrived."

I swore.

"I'll do my best to stall them, but you might want to get out of there soon," Heather said.

"Thanks for the heads-up."

Well, now I was on a timeline. I scootched on my stomach close to the two power outlets. The one on the left looked normal and even had a light plugged into it. But on closer inspection, the one on the right looked a bit strange; it was tilted just a couple of degrees. I wedged my fingernails underneath the plate and gently pulled it back from the wall.

"Bingo," I muttered to myself. There hadn't been an outlet here at all. Rex had simply carved a hole in the drywall and placed an empty plate there. I reached inside and pulled out a small thumb drive. This was exactly what I needed.

Because I knew the feds were on their way, and I wasn't sure how long Heather would manage to stall them, I shoved the thumb drive inside my bra for safekeeping and started planning my escape.

Chapter 12

I couldn't go out the front door. Well, I supposed I could. Who had called the feds here? It was probably that nosy New Yorker from down the hall. I thought the whole thing about New York was you were supposed to mind your own business if you saw something weird happening.

If she had called them, then there was no point in my hiding my presence anymore. They would have known I was here.

But if she hadn't, then by going back out through the front, I risked getting caught.

I approached the front door but heard voices from the other side. "Yeah, I spoke to that lady the other day when we were here. She doesn't know anything. One of those crazy old broads who doesn't have anything interesting going on in her life, so she has to meddle in other people's affairs. It doesn't surprise me one bit that she called us. I bet she just saw someone from housekeeping walk past and figured that someone with vaguely dark skin meant they were up to no good then made up this story about someone coming in through the balcony."

I paused, the blood turning to ice in my veins. These were the feds, and they were right outside the door. The old lady had called them after all.

I was about to take a step back when I suddenly heard her voice.

"Oh, good, you gentlemen have finally arrived. It took you long enough. Where did you start from, Los Angeles? I called you nearly forty-five minutes ago. I could have driven to the other side of the island and back in that time."

"All right, ma'am, well, we're here now," one of the feds told her.

"Yes, well, congratulations. So is the heat death of the entire universe, given how long this whole thing took you. That's if you believe in all this climate change stuff you see on the news, anyway."

I bit back a smile as I realized that the old lady being out here meant her room would be empty. I turned and darted back to the balcony. All I had to do was get over to her balcony and pass through her room and out to the stairwell without being spotted. Given that the woman's room was located right next to the stairwell, it was my best shot at getting out of here without getting caught.

It wasn't the best plan in the world, but then again, neither was creating Jurassic Park, and that went all right in the end. Sort of. Okay, bad example.

This time, the fear of being arrested and thrown into a black hole in Guantanamo for the rest of my life overtook my fear of the gap between the aluminum railings, and I launched myself back across the two balconies until I was on the old lady's. I pulled the door and was eternally grateful to find it unlocked.

I ran into her hotel suite and back to the front door, then slowly cracked it open just an inch. I could still hear her talking to the feds outside.

"Are you going to go in? You've been standing out here for five minutes."

"Ma'am, respectfully, that's because you haven't stopped talking since we got here," one of the FBI agents said, obviously exasperated.

"There was nothing respectful about that sentence," the old lady snapped.

"Look, can you just go back to your room so we can do our job?" the other agent said, his voice tinged with the kind of irritated tone one used with a small child who wasn't doing what they were supposed to.

This was my last chance. If I didn't leave now, odds were good I'd be caught.

I slipped out of the room as quietly as I could then opened the stairwell door. Of course, it opened with a clunk.

"Hey, you!" one of the FBI agents called out.

Well, so much for getting out without being seen.

I pretended not to hear and entered the stairwell. As soon as I was out of sight of the door, I began sprinting down the stairs. The echo of my feet slapping along the concrete steps reverberated across the narrow space. A moment later, it was joined by the sound of the stairwell door flying open.

I was being chased by the FBI.

I sprinted down the stairs as fast as I could, my heart thundering against my chest in a combination of fear and exertion. I had to get down ten flights of stairs. If I could just get to the lobby before my pursuers, I could dump the wig and sunglasses, and hopefully, they wouldn't recognize me.

I should have worn some sort of reversible jacket.

As I reached the fifth-floor landing, I turned to look up and see how much of a lead I still had on the two agents and what the odds were that they were going to catch me. The next thing I knew, I collided with someone, knocking a breath out of me.

I stumbled, but two hands grabbed me around the waist, and I looked up to find myself staring right into Jake's eyes. His brow furrowed in confusion.

"Charlie? What are you doing here?" he asked.

I looked up the stairwell to where the FBI agents were hot on my tail. "You have to help me," I begged in a quiet whisper. "Don't let them arrest me. I don't want to die in some hole in like, Arkansas."

Jake raised his eyebrows. "I don't think the FBI is going to kill you."

"Please," I begged. "I'm too sexy for jail."

"Okay, Right Said Fred," Jake muttered as the sound of the agents' footsteps came closer. "I'll get you out of here. Turn around. You're under arrest."

I did as Jake asked, and a moment later, I felt the cool metal of handcuffs on my wrists. They clacked shut at the same time as I heard one of the agents speak.

"Hand her over. She's wanted for questioning."

I turned and finally got a good look at the two agents. They were both men in their late thirties. The one on the left was obviously the one who had just spoken. He was around six foot two and had his sandy hair in a slicked-back side part. He had a thin runner's frame and had obviously suffered a lot less on that run down the stairs than his partner had. The other man was about the same height but easily carried an extra fifty pounds. He leaned against the railing, breathing heavily, his round face doing a great impression of a tomato.

Both men wore dark, short-sleeved shirts with FBI emblazoned on the chest in yellow and long pants despite the wardrobe being completely inappropriate for the climate.

Jake pulled out his badge. "Detective Jake Llewelyn, Maui Police. This woman is under arrest; I've been after her for a long time."

"Well, we're FBI," said the agent who looked like his lungs hadn't completely given out on him, pulling out his own badge. "Agent Andrew Forrester, and this is Agent Jonathan Sparks. We're going to have to take your suspect in for questioning."

"Sorry, guys. I don't know how it works over on Oahu, but I've made this arrest, and I've called it in, and my captain is going to be real mad if I don't bring in a criminal I've been trying to get off the streets for six months after I've let him know she's in custody.

And trust me, I'm more afraid of him than I am of you."

"She's wanted for questioning with regard to a break and enter in one of the hotel rooms here," Agent Sparks finally managed to spit out.

"There was a break-in up there?" Jake asked, his eyebrows raised.

"Bull," I said with a laugh. "I heard the conversation the two of you had with that old lady. You never even went into that room. I wasn't there, but you have no idea either way."

The two agents shared a look.

"She's not lying," Jake said, incredulous. "You just tried to steal my arrest so you could talk to her about something you're not sure is a crime."

"We're talking about a murder investigation here. What do you have her on?"

"Well, she's got a long list of complaints against her. Public urination, mostly," Jake replied with a grin.

I glared at him. I was going to kill him when we got out of here. Public urination? *Really*? He was totally embarrassing me on purpose.

"At least twelve counts. Oh, and three counts of indecent exposure. And those are just the ones we have on record."

I was *totally* going to kill him.

"That's nothing compared to murder," Agent Forrester said.

"Sure. But it sounds to me like you don't have any grounds to arrest her. Look, I'm going to take her in, because I have an actual crime to charge her with. If you want to talk to her after she's released on bail, be my guest. But you can't have my criminal because you think she might have been near the scene of something you don't even know is a crime. Do you actually have anything that links her to your murder?"

"No," Agent Sparks admitted, earning himself a glare from his partner.

"Well, there you have it. Talk to my captain, John Mueller. Have a great day, gentlemen."

"Don't you know who we are?" Agent Forrester interrupted. "We're the feds. Our investigation is more important than yours, which means we get to take her."

Jake laughed. "I don't know what kind of bull they teach you out there in Quantico, but you're a long way from there, and that's not how things work on this island. As I said, call my captain."

And with that, Jake gave me a gentle tug toward the door leading to the fifth floor. We marched down the hall in silence, the ding of the elevator's arrival the only sound breaking the awkward tension between us. We had to be thinking about the same thing: last night.

Finally, as the enclosed metal box lurched downward, I had had enough, and I turned to Jake. "Public urination, huh?"

He grinned, and the tension between us dissolved like cotton candy in a puddle. "Hey, if you want me to save you from getting questioned by the feds, you can't complain if I want to have a little bit of fun."

"For the record, if I *was* a criminal, I would commit way cooler crimes."

He raised an eyebrow skyward as the doors opened,

and we stepped back out into the lobby and headed toward the parking lot. "Like breaking and entering? I desperately want to know what you think a "cool" crime is."

"Stealing from rich people," I replied immediately. "Not like, just kind of rich, either. Owns-a-castle-in-France rich. Hunts-homeless-people-for-sport rich."

"That's the plot of a Jean-Claude Van Damme movie, not real life."

"We can't know that for sure. I met a guy who qualifies for that rich the other day. Anyway, you wanted my answer? There's my answer. I'd totally be a criminal who would steal a Fabergé egg from a billionaire with a castle. Then, I'd sell it to a museum and donate the proceeds to good causes. I'd basically be Robin Hood is what I'm saying."

"What kind of museum would buy a Fabergé egg that's recently been reported stolen?"

I shook my head. "You're not thinking this through. The billionaire can't report the egg stolen, because that would draw attention to himself and his hunting-people-for-sport hobby. So he just lets it go, and the museum has no idea. Until I release the video footage of it that I took at the same time, and he's arrested, and his assets are seized, and they give me the Nobel Peace Prize."

"This isn't the first time you've considered this scenario, is it?" he asked, raising a single eyebrow again. "Anyway, come on. I'm going to drive you out of here in case the feds are still watching."

Jake led me to his car and removed the handcuffs

from my wrists as soon as I was in the back seat. "What are you doing here, anyway? Why were you in that stairwell?" I asked.

"Following up on another totally unrelated investigation. It's a small island. What about you? Actually, you know what? I don't want to know. I'm just going to assume you did exactly what the feds wanted to question you about, and we'll leave it at that. I don't want to make myself an accessory to the long list of crimes I'm sure you've just committed."

"That's probably a good call. For what it's worth, I didn't do anything actually *bad*."

"Oh, well, that makes me feel a lot better," Jake said sarcastically. "I swear, why do I let you rope me into your insane life? Do you know how many people I know who have been chased by *federal agents* down a stairwell at a luxury hotel? One. I don't even have to think about it. It's *one*."

"My mother always said to be unique," I replied, leaning back against the seat as Jake drove off. "Where are you taking me? Please don't tell me you're actually arresting me."

"Believe me, I'm tempted. But no, I have an actual job to do that doesn't involve bailing you out. Where are you parked?"

"The public lot just down the street. Thanks."

Jake drove along, and the awkwardness between us returned. I couldn't help but think about what had happened the last time we were in a car like this together. Luckily, the ride only lasted about a minute before he pulled up in front of Queenie.

"Right," I said, clearing my throat. "Thanks for, uh, bailing me out back there. Although if you hadn't been in my way, I totally would have beat them down to the lobby and gotten away."

"I'm sure you would have. You're welcome."

"Are you going to get in trouble with your boss?"

Jake laughed. "If there's one thing movies and TV get right, it's the petty rivalry between local cops and the feds. They wanted to steal someone they thought I was actually arresting out from under my nose? Well, my captain is very much going to enjoy telling them to shove it. Liam is going to enjoy this story too."

"Yeah, I bet. Where is he, anyway? Stuck trying to decide between a Boston Cream and an éclair?"

"Running late, and *not* because of donuts," Jake replied, shooting me a look. "I figured I'd get my interview started without him, but now I'm running late too."

"Look on the bright side: you saved an innocent resident of Maui from a cruel fate today."

"Happy to be of service. And by that, I mean for goodness' sake, Charlie, stay away from the feds."

"I will."

I climbed out of the car and immediately dumped the wig and sunglasses in a nearby garbage can before heading back to Queenie. I wasn't stupid enough to let myself get caught with that kind of evidence if the two agents happened to come by.

I hopped into Queenie and decided to make myself scarce just in case. I was driving along the highway, trying to decide if I wanted to pull off at Leoda's to get a pie for the trip home, when my phone started ringing.

That settled it; I had to pull off to answer it, so I might as well get a pie while I was at it. Those were the rules. I swiped my finger across the screen to answer as I pulled into one of the parking spots, a hen squawking at me in annoyance as she moved slowly out of the way.

"Hello?"

"Hi, Charlie," Heather's voice chirped on the other end of the line. "I was just calling to make sure you were all right. I saw you being led away; do you need help?"

"Oh, thanks, but I'm good. That was a, uh, friend of mine, just getting me away from the FBI." Friend? What was Jake to me? Random guy I made out with like twelve hours earlier? I shoved the thought from my head, which was tough, because as soon as the memory flooded back, a wave of heat washed over me, rolling through my core.

"Good. I've also been able to secure you a position at the rehearsal dinner tonight if you think that will help. You'll be acting as my personal assistant, which will get you access to everyone you can think of. There's nobody people are more eager to help than a new widow. It begins at seven in the main ballroom. Formal dress, of course."

"I'll be there," I said. But first, I needed to get to Dot's place and have a look at what was on that thumb drive.

Chapter 13

By the time I pulled into Dot's apartment building, I had pie crumbs all over my face, and the adrenaline in my body had cooled down. I was finally able to think a little bit more clearly. That wasn't how I'd planned on seeing Jake. I hadn't planned on seeing him at all, ever again.

But now it had happened, and I had to admit, it wasn't as awkward as I thought it was going to be. Maybe I was growing up a little after all.

I knocked on Dot's door. I pulled the thumb drive from my bra when she answered it and wiggled it with a grin.

"Well, I guess there are worse places you could have hidden that, though I'm not the biggest fan of boob sweat," Dot said, raising her eyebrows and holding a palm out. "Where'd you find it?"

"Hidden behind a fake electrical outlet near the desk Rex was using. And my boobs don't sweat."

Rosie, standing at the kitchen counter and drinking a glass of water, looked impressed. "Good find."

"Thanks. I'm better than the feds. Although they almost arrested me. Hence the hiding-the-key-in-the-bra thing."

"Luckily, you got away. Now, let's see what's on this thing."

Instead of going to her main machine, Dot moved to the living room and pulled a laptop from the drawer underneath a side table.

"How many computers do you own?" I asked.

"Right now, I have about ten in this apartment. This one is air-gapped. That means it's never been connected to the internet. It doesn't even have the capability to do it; I removed the wireless card and the ethernet connection before it was ever turned on."

"Why are you using that one to look at the thumb drive?"

"Because I don't know what's on it. Given its origins and Rex's history, there's a chance that this drive has software or files on it designed to corrupt the computer that opens it or to disrupt my network. So I'm opening it on a computer that has no exterior access. The files on this are encrypted too, so it's going to take a few minutes for me to get through that."

"Don't take too long. I'm going to the wedding rehearsal dinner tonight as Heather's personal assistant. It starts at seven, and I have to find something appropriate to wear. Which is code for raiding Zoe's closet."

"You'll have plenty of time. I just got in."

I walked over to the couch and plonked myself

down next to Dot, who opened a folder full of files. "I wonder what's on here. It has to be important. Nobody encrypts a thumb drive and hides it behind a fake outlet they put into a hotel room over nothing."

Dot double clicked the first file, a PDF, and the screen immediately opened a blueprint.

"What's that of?" I asked, squinting at the screen and trying to get a good look.

Dot zoomed in on part of the screen, and we were able to better make it out.

"It looks like infrastructure plans. For a power plant, by the looks," Rosie said.

Terror wrapped itself around me like the world's least comforting hug as realization dawned upon me. "There's no reason for Rex to have anything like this, and certainly even less reason to hide it, unless he was doing something bad with it."

Dot's mouth was a grim line as she turned to face me. "It appears our Soviet spy came out of his retirement."

"The question is, who is he working for, and are they the ones who killed him?" Rosie said. "Let me have a look at these files. I want to see what they are."

Dot handed the laptop over, and Rosie began scanning all of the files on the drive.

"These are all buildings in New York State important to infrastructure," she announced. "Power plants, rail systems, water reservoirs, that sort of thing."

"Are you thinking whoever wants this information is thinking about terrorism?" I asked.

Rosie pursed her lips as she considered her answer.

Eventually, she replied slowly. "I don't think so. I think it's more likely the plans are going to be sold to someone who intends to use them for ransom purposes. But it's possible I'm wrong. Either way, this thumb drive was well hidden, and Heather didn't know anything about it, did she?"

"I don't think so," I replied. "But I think she suspected her husband if nothing else. She told me she purposely kept a bit of a blind eye when it came to him. That tells me that even if it was on a subconscious level, she thought something was up with him."

"This proves that, yes, indeed. The question is, what? Did Rex plan to meet a buyer here on Maui? Did the deal go south, and Rex ended up bashed over the head?"

"That would seem to me to be most likely. Otherwise, what are the other options? Someone from the CIA found out about what he was doing and decided that rather than throw him in a hole somewhere that he'd never come out of, they'd just end him? I don't know."

"That didn't happen; the CIA would be cleaner than that," Rosie replied. "I think the buyer theory is a much better one."

"Okay. Heather thinks the FBI was called in because the CIA somehow knew about this, and they can't be seen investigating on American soil."

"That would make sense, especially given what we've found," Rosie replied. "What we don't know is whether Rex was working with them, or if they were secretly following his every move to find his buyer."

"So now we just have to find out who Rex was trying to meet with to sell his information," I said. "That should be super easy. On the bright side, we still don't have any proof that Rex was going to involve Rosie in any of this."

"Not yet. I don't like the fact that he was still involved in stuff that could, at the very, least be considered spy adjacent," Rosie said. "It's very possible his buyer is someone working for a foreign country directly. Frankly, I'd be much happier if it turned out that the crime was as simple as Chet being unable to repay his future father-in-law and wanting to erase the debt by erasing its owner."

"Me too. Well, I'll see what I can find out tonight. I'd better get home and find something appropriate to wear before I have to go back up to Ka'anapali." I stood up from the couch. "I'll leave you with the thumb drive. Let me know if you find anything else relevant on it, will you?"

"Will do," Dot said.

AT QUARTER TO SEVEN, I WAS WALKING THROUGH the lobby of the Beach Dreams Resort once more. I'd found a floral-print maxi dress that reached down to my calves, black with emerald green leaves and dotted with white hibiscus flowers. I paired it with a thick brown leather belt and a matching clutch. White sandals completed the outfit, which probably would have been considered casual on the mainland but was perfectly appropriate for a formal dinner on Hawaii.

I entered through the lobby and passed by the main bar to the left as I headed toward Mahi Ai, the restaurant hosting the rehearsal dinner. I glanced inside as I passed and stopped dead in my tracks.

Seated at the bar, laughing at a joke told by a man who was most definitely not Sean, was Samantha.

I paused, stopping to have a look. Samantha was dressed in a low-cut top, her hair and makeup pristine. I could only see the man she was speaking to from the back, but his round, bald head and pudgy frame immediately told me there was no way it was Sean. Samantha seemed to be genuinely flirting with the man.

Was this what had set Sean off? Did he know she was cheating on him?

I frowned. I had to get to the dinner, but I made a mental note to stop back here later and speak with the bartender. I needed some answers.

Continuing to Mahi Ai, I entered the restaurant and announced to the hostess that I was here for the rehearsal dinner.

"Great. We've got your party seated in our private section upstairs. If you'll please follow me."

The hostess led me through the modern restaurant and up a set of stairs to the private mezzanine level of the restaurant. At the top of the stairs was an A-frame chalkboard sign with the hashtag the couple were using for the wedding, #YouveBeenThunderStruck, drawn on it, along with invitations to use it on all social media accounts. The space had enough room for about fifty guests, with tables set up with name tags. At the front of the room was a long table for the bridal party, and behind them was a balcony that overlooked the beach.

The décor was modern, with dark hardwood floors, wood tables, and leather-upholstered chairs. Tea lights floated in small containers of water set at the center of every table, and can lights embedded in the high ceiling added to the lighting offered by the contemporary geometric chandeliers.

About twenty people were already here, mingling with one another. I scanned the space, looking for Heather. I found her speaking with a man in the corner. Heather was dressed in a simple black suit, which worked surprisingly well as an appropriate choice of clothing for this event as both a rehearsal dinner and newly widowed grieving wife.

I walked toward her, and as soon as she spotted me, she smiled.

"Ah, Charlotte," she exclaimed, motioning me over. "Let me introduce you to Alan, the general manager here at the resort."

Everything about Alan was medium. Middle-aged, about five foot ten, medium build, with brown hair styled the way every single man around his age seemed to keep it. He wore a full suit and carried himself with the confidence of a man who knew every inch of this hotel and the way it was operated.

"Hi, Alan. It's nice to meet you," I said, shaking his hand. As expected, his handshake was firm without being overly aggressive.

"Charlotte here is working for me temporarily as a personal assistant. I'm very grateful to her for taking me on as a client at the last minute. As you must understand, Alan, the last few days have just been so difficult. And with Melissa's wedding going ahead, I have to be able to be there for my daughter. It's a lot for me to handle at once, so Charlotte is taking a few things off my plate while she can."

"Of course," Alan said with a smile.

"Now, if you'll excuse me, I must go speak with Melissa."

Heather headed off and left me alone with the hotel manager.

"It's such a tragedy," Alan said, shaking his head. "I can't believe it."

"Did you know Heather and Rex?" I asked him.

"Yes; I used to manage our Manhattan property. Rex was involved in a real estate deal concerning the land about ten years ago. I met him then, and of course as soon as he arrived here, I reintroduced myself. What with the number of guests that they have staying with us this week, I wanted them to know I was available to them personally for whatever they required. And then, of course, Rex's life was tragically ended. It's horrible. The FBI have been called in; they're on the case. I'm sure they'll get to the bottom of this."

"Do you know why it's them and not the regular police that are investigating?"

"I imagine Rex must have known enough people to have some strings pulled. He was one of the most well-known real estate investors in New York. That's only a guess though."

"Did you ever see Rex meeting with anybody who wasn't part of the wedding party while he was here? Maybe someone he seemed to be doing business with?"

The slightest crease formed between Alan's eyes. "No. Why would you ask that?"

"Oh, when I was with Heather earlier, speaking with the agents in charge of the case, they wanted to know about Rex's movements in the days before his death. Heather was distressed; after they left, she wanted me to tell her if I spoke to anyone who might have known what Rex did in the last few days, to help the FBI solve his murder. I've been asking around for her, as it's obviously much less painful for me to do so."

"Right. That makes sense. That poor woman. I can't imagine how she must be feeling. She's so strong. Actually, you know what? Now that I think about it, I did see Rex with somebody. It was, uh, the night before he died. Wednesday night, around nine. He was at the bar, speaking with a person I didn't recognize."

"Can you describe them for me?"

Alan shifted his weight to his other foot. "Not really, no. Sorry. He had his back to me. But he was male. Black hair. Kind of average build. That's all I can tell you."

That was too bad. This could have been the kind of break in the case I needed.

"Okay, thanks. Is there anything else you can tell me about Rex that might be important? I can pass it on to the feds without having to worry Heather."

"No. I don't have a clue. Frankly, I have trouble believing this could have been anything other than a random attack. Who would have wanted to kill Rex? He wasn't the kind of man to have enemies, and he didn't know anyone on the island other than his friends and family who are here for the wedding."

"And the man you saw him with at the bar," I pointed out.

"Right. But Rex was a good man. He was a good businessman, but a fair one. And that's not something that's guaranteed these days. He'll be missed, but I'm afraid I can't help the feds. Or Heather. I don't know who could have done this."

"Okay, thanks," I said. "I appreciate it."

"Enjoy the dinner. If you'll excuse me, I have to get back to my desk."

Alan left, and before I could so much as turn around, I felt a presence next to me.

"You must be Heather's new assistant. She didn't mention how gorgeous you are."

I turned and found myself looking at Chet Struckman.

Chapter 14

He looked exactly how he did on his video, only dressed more like a normal human being than a wannabe character in the next iteration of *Street Fighter*. Wearing a navy-blue polo with beige slacks, Chet looked surprisingly normal here tonight compared to the bro I'd seen on the YouTube video.

"And what's your name?" he asked.

"Charlotte," I said, following Heather's lead in announcing myself using my real name. "And I know you. You're Chet. You know, the guy with a fiancée?"

His smile didn't waver so much as an inch. "Oh, come on. I might be about to be married, but I'm only human. I can compliment a beautiful woman. So, you're working for Heather, are you? What exactly are you doing for her? It's not like she has a lot on her plate right now. Melissa is fine handling all the wedding stuff, and there's nothing to do about poor Rex until they fly his body back to New York, and that's going to be after an autopsy."

"I've been hired to protect her interests and to act as a liaison between her and the agents working Rex's case so that she doesn't have to stress herself out too much by worrying about who killed her husband."

"Well, good luck with that. If you ask me, it's a local who probably tried to mug him and got angry when Rex refused."

"You think Rex wouldn't have given up the money?"

Chet snorted. "No, of course not. Dude had balls of steel. He was old school. You know, what these social-justice-warrior lefties today would call a toxic male. But he just knew how to stand up for himself. And he was a great businessman. Wouldn't take a no from anybody."

"What about when you told him you couldn't pay him back for the loans he gave your business?"

This time, the smile did drop from Chet's face. "How on earth do you know about that? Did Heather tell you?"

"So it's true."

"No. I'm just having temporary cash flow problems. It's a big issue when you're growing a business, you know?" Chet puffed out his chest to look important. "I could have gone the VC route. You know, I have a line with Marc Cuban. And Rex is good friends with Barbara, of course. I could have gotten one of the sharks from *Shark Tank* to invest with me, but I wanted to maintain control of my company.

When it's worth billions, every percentage point is going to count. So yeah, I went to Rex, and I laid things out for him, and I showed him how we're disrupting the fitness industry. He gave me some money, but he understood that it would be a while before I paid him back. I'm taking an aggressive growth strategy. That's going to involve being lean for a few years, but I know what I'm doing. I might look like a dumb jock, but it's just an act. I went to Wharton."

"Does that mean Rex wasn't asking you to pay him back right away?"

"Nah, he knows the drill. A good business, it's got to lose money before it can make money, you know? Well, you probably don't."

"Right, I didn't go to Wharton," I said dryly. "I went to school where they teach you that when you run out of money, that's it, you go out of business."

"That's poor-people talk," Chet replied, shaking his head.

This was why I didn't carry a Taser around. If anybody deserved to get "accidentally" zapped tonight, it was this guy.

"No, if you want the reward, you have to take the risk. And sometimes, that means debt. But Rex understood that. That's why he had so much cash. He took those risks back in the eighties and nineties. A ton of people went broke around then. They gave up, but Rex saw opportunity. And that's what he saw in me too. If you're trying to insinuate that I killed him over that cash, you're wrong. And if you go to the feds and tell them that, I'll ruin your life. Do you know who my dad is?"

"No, but I bet he went to Wharton."

"Damn right he did. And look, it's not his fault that the economy collapsed in the nineties and he lost a lot of what he had, but there are certain circles where the Struckman family name still carries a lot of weight."

I raised my eyebrows. "You belong to *that* Struckman family?"

Back in the seventies and eighties, the Struckmans had been about a rung below the Kennedys when it came to importance. At one point, both New York State senators were Struckmans. In fact, the family patriarch, Samuel Struckman, had been rumored to be a presidential hopeful in the 1992 election. Unfortunately, when the real estate market crashed in the late eighties, the family ended up losing a whole lot of its fortune. I didn't know the details, what with not having been born at the time, but Mom and Dad had talked about it a bit in my childhood, and it became part of the cultural Zeitgeist. A family on top of the world that lost everything.

Of course, when you have *that* much money, losing everything means you still have millions of dollars, a pad in Manhattan, and a country house in the Hamptons. But their political careers were finished almost overnight, and they never regained the level of prestige the name used to carry.

"That's right," Chet said with a smarmy smile. "So be careful what you say to me."

I snorted. "Yeah, you must be just full of influence

if you had to go to your fiancée's daddy for money to fund your company."

"It's not my fault my father is an idiot who couldn't manage his money properly and can't see an opportunity when it slaps him in the face. It's not enough that he squandered the money that should have been my inheritance, but then when I ask for a measly four hundred grand to start my company, he has the gall to tell me my business idea is terrible? Believe me, I wouldn't have killed Rex. He believed in me when my own father didn't."

"It sounds like Wharton really paid off for him."

Before I had a chance to say anything further, the bride appeared. Melissa Thunder was nothing short of drop-dead gorgeous. Her silver heels had her standing at nearly six feet, and she was sheathed in a figure-hugging black dress that showed off her slender body and subtle curvature. Diamonds studs in her ears and around her neck glimmered in the light, giving her a slightly ethereal look. She carried herself like a woman who knew her worth in the world and wasn't afraid of anybody.

"Chet, darling, are you speaking to Mom's new assistant and you're not introducing me?" she said with a teasing smile. She held out a hand for me to shake, which I did. "I'm Melissa Thunder."

"Charlotte Gibson. It's nice to meet you."

"And you. Thank you for everything you're doing for my mother. Chet, do be a dear and speak with Randall Chase, would you? He's been telling me all night how he wants to get your opinion about something related to protein drinks."

"Will do, doll. You know there's nothing I like talking about more than my whey powder." He kissed Melissa on the cheek and flashed me a wink as he left.

I looked over to gauge whether Melissa had seen it, but if she had, she obviously couldn't have cared less.

"So, you're obviously investigating Dad's murder for my mom. What are you thinking? Is Chet a suspect?" Melissa asked. She must have noticed the stunned expression that crossed my face, because she continued. "Oh, come on. I wasn't born yesterday. Chet might not know how to use Google, but I do. You're not a personal assistant, you're a private investigator. And Mom is the most organized person in the world and thrives in a crisis. She doesn't need someone to help her through this. So what else would she hire you for? Because she doesn't trust those morons from the FBI, and I want to actually get closure. So tell me: do you suspect Chet? Because I swear, if he ruins all of this for me by having murdered my dad, I will kill him myself."

"Yes, he is a suspect, but he's not the main suspect. Your father loaned him money to start his business, and Chet is borderline bankrupt. I think there's a chance Chet killed him so he wouldn't have to repay the money." Melissa was obviously the kind of woman who didn't beat around the bush or accept any bull, so I figured I'd meet that energy.

Melissa snorted. "Chet idolized Dad. He saw him as the kind of businessman his own father wasn't. He wouldn't have killed him. Besides, Dad was fine with loaning him the money. He had plenty more where that came from, and he wanted this marriage to happen as much as I do. I certainly think Chet could be dumb enough to kill someone, but if he did kill my dad, you're missing the motive entirely."

"Okay, so I'm going to state the obvious here, but you don't seem to be particularly enamored of your fiancé."

Melissa looked around and lowered her voice. "You're not wrong. I'll deny any of this if you repeat it, but in the interest of helping you find who killed my dad, I'll tell you the truth. Chet is a moron with one single lonely brain cell in that empty head, and even it heads out most of the time. I'm not marrying him because I love him. I'm marrying him because I love my career and my social standing more than anything. I'm the accident late-in-life daughter of two poor people who grew up in Brooklyn. He managed to win the genetic lottery to be born into one of the most famous families in the whole country. As Melissa Thunder, I'm editor-in-chief at an architecture magazine. But as Melissa Struckman, that name alone opens doors."

Melissa leaned in toward me, and a gleam of ambition flashed in her eyes. "I could be the next Anna Wintour. Can you imagine? Because I do. Every night. And marrying Chet is like taking the elevator while everyone else is scrambling to get up the ladder."

"And here I thought marriages of convenience were a thing of the past."

"Not for me. Not right now. I'm using this marriage to get what I want in life. That's more important to me than spending time with someone I love. I don't have time for that right now anyway."

"Okay. So you don't think Chet murdered Rex?"

"No. For all his bravado and cocky exterior, I don't think Chet has it in him. Besides, Dad knew how important this was to me. And it's not like he couldn't afford to lose the money. I'm pretty sure he knew going into it that Chet's business was eventually going to fail, and he would never get it back. I mean come on. Testosterzone? Really? He wouldn't have pressured Chet to repay him. Especially not now, so close to the wedding."

"Do you know who could have killed your dad?" I asked as softly as I could.

Melissa's eyes misted over, and she swallowed hard and blinked rapidly a few times. "No," she finally said, her voice still strong. She reminded me a lot of Heather. "I'm afraid I don't. But then, I only spoke to my parents once a week. I wasn't privy to a lot of their lives. They love me though. Dad loved me. He was so helpful. I never told them, but I know he recognized that I didn't really love Chet. He knew what was going on, but he hid it. He still did everything he could. He paid for the whole wedding. He even made a Pinterest board for me, where he would put all sorts of stuff he thought I'd like. He researched all the cake vendors for me. He's the one who suggested this hotel. We spent one night going through potential photographers' portfolios together on FaceTime. He was wonderful. I can't imagine who would have wanted Dad dead or why they'd be here in Hawaii.

"I'm sorry. I wish I could help more. If you need anything at all, please let me know. I know Mom has hired you, and I will do whatever you need if it'll help catch Dad's killer."

"Thank you for the offer. I'll let you know."

"I can't believe he was killed two days before my wedding day," Melissa said, her voice hollow as she stared off into the distance, her eyes unfocused. "He was supposed to walk me down the aisle tomorrow. Now that's not happening. Mom is going to do it. She's so proud. But we both know it's not the same."

"I'm really sorry about your dad. I know how hard it is to lose one."

Melissa's eyes darted to mine. "I'm sorry too. For you. You're about the same age as I am, which means you lost your dad earlier."

"I was sixteen. You won't forget him. The pain never goes away entirely. Small things will always remind you of him, but it does get easier. That crushing feeling in your chest will subside eventually. But that doesn't help you now."

"No. It doesn't, but it still helps to know there's a light at the end of the tunnel. I appreciate your kind words. And I'm telling you, if you need anything at all, please let me know. I want justice for Dad. His killer deserves to rot in jail. Are you staying for dinner?"

I nodded. "Yes."

"Good. I believe the first course is being served in

ten minutes. Now, if you'll excuse me, I've got to do my rounds."

"Absolutely."

I watched as Melissa sauntered off, looking after her curiously. She reminded me a lot of Heather with her straightforward manner. It was interesting that she'd said both her parents had grown up in Brooklyn; obviously neither of them had told her the truth about their past.

Was she right about Chet? Was he really too much of a coward to kill Rex? And was Rex really fine with losing that much money just so his daughter could marry into a prestigious family?

I had to admit, it sounded plausible. Weird but plausible. And if that was the case, that took us back to Rex and his mystery business deal relating to the thumb drive behind the outlet.

But how on earth was I supposed to find some sort of mystery person Rex was dealing with?

That was the question I had to answer.

Chapter 15

When Melissa left, Heather approached me and led me gently by the arm into a corner.

"I saw you speaking with Chet. What do you think?"

"I still haven't ruled him out as a suspect. Listen, this afternoon, when I was in your room, I found something."

Heather's spine stiffened slightly, but her expression remained flat. "Yes? What was it?"

"A hidden thumb drive. I haven't been through all of the files on it, but they appear to be infrastructure related, in New York state."

Heather closed her eyes and blew out a sigh. "I was afraid of that. I didn't want to believe it, but…"

I replied. "You suspected though. You purposely closed your eyes to it."

"If I'm honest, yes. I didn't want to know. And I didn't know for sure. But you must understand, it was for my own mental health. I couldn't have that hanging over me again. Rex was always more of a risk taker than I was. He was the kind of man who, after the wall came down, would have started looking for new opportunities, thinking that we were forgotten. But when I saw the FBI were assigned to his case, I knew. I knew he was into something, because the feds don't get involved in regular murder cases. And that means I have to stay at arm's length as well, because I don't want them knowing about *me*."

"Understood, of course. I think Rex was meeting with someone here, on the island. A buyer of the information he had or a middleman maybe? Either way, do you know who it could have been? Did he mention seeing someone? Did you see him with somebody, maybe someone you didn't think of at the time?"

Heather shook her head. "Sorry. I've been racking my brain, trying to think, but I really did turn a blind eye to things. And Rex might have been a little bit reckless, but he wasn't an idiot. He would have known to keep this from me as much as he could, and he still knew what he was doing. If he really wanted to keep this from anybody, including me, he could have done so."

"Do you know anyone on the island?"

"No. I've never been to Hawaii. I don't know anyone here beyond the locals I've met the last few days who are working for the wedding. I didn't think Rex did, either. He certainly never mentioned anybody."

"Who do you have working for the wedding who are local?"

"The main photographer, for one. That's her over there, snapping photos." Heather motioned with her head, and I turned to see an Asian woman with straight black hair tied back into a ponytail. She was short and slim and dressed in neutral beige, which helped her blend into the background. She darted around the room like a sparrow, the shutter of her camera clicking away every few seconds. "She's a hard worker. I like her. But Rex wouldn't have known her; Melissa chose her."

"What about you and Rex? Was there anyone here you were involved with before the wedding?"

"The planner did almost everything," Heather said, shaking her head. "Rex spoke about some of this with Melissa, but he never came out here. And besides, Melissa wouldn't have known anything about this. Anyone they spoke about would have just been a wedding vendor. I just don't know. I wish I did."

"It's all right. I've still got some leads to follow," I lied. "Now if you'll excuse me, I need to duck out for a moment before dinner is served."

WHILE I TRIED TO FIGURE OUT MY NEXT STEPS, I decided to take the ten minutes before dinner started to sneak down to the bar to get some answers about Samantha and who she was seeing. After all, maybe I had it all wrong. Maybe she wasn't cheating on Sean at all, but there was a completely innocent explanation.

I doubted it though.

By the time I reached the bar, Samantha had disappeared, and so had the man she was with. I sidled my way up onto one of the stools and caught the bartender's eye. He looked like an ex-army type—broad-shouldered with a shaved head—who could probably double as a bouncer if necessary.

When he spoke, I did a double take at his British accent. I hadn't been expecting that.

"What can I get for you there, love?"

"Whatever you've got on tap, and a bit of information," I said. I realized I didn't have a picture of Samantha on my phone. "There was a woman in here earlier with a man, sitting at the bar here. She's blond, pretty."

"Oh, sure. Yeah, I remember them," he said as he grabbed a glass and poured my beer. "They just left a couple minutes ago. What do you want to know about them for? You a cop?"

"No, I'm a friend of hers. I couldn't stop to say hi, so I texted her, but she hasn't replied. I'm just a bit worried about her, because I didn't recognize the man she was with. Do you know who he was?"

"Well, I'm not really supposed to give you this information," the bartender said.

I changed my expression to one of worry. "Please. I'm worried about her. I don't want to call the cops in case she's totally fine and I'm overreacting. But if not..."

I let my voice trail off. I was sure the bartender could use his imagination. It wouldn't go well for him if a young woman's body was found in this hotel and it was later determined that someone specifically told him they were worried for her safety and he chose to do nothing.

"Okay, look," the bartender said, glancing around nervously and lowering his voice. "I don't want anything to happen to your friend. So you didn't hear this from me, but the guy who was with your friend, he charged the items on the bill to room 614."

"Thanks," I said, sliding him a twenty. "Enjoy the beer."

I left the bar and immediately headed to the elevator bank. The metal tube flew upward toward the sixth floor, and I realized I had no idea at all what I was doing. What was the plan here? Just knock on the door and go, "Hi, I know I'm probably interrupting something happening between the sheets, but I've been spying on the woman in there because her mechanic suspects her boyfriend is abusive, so can someone tell me what's going on here?"

No, that was ridiculous. I was being ridiculous. Samantha was an adult woman who was allowed to make her own decisions. Besides, just because she had left the bar with the man didn't mean they had immediately come back up here to his hotel room. She could have just gone back to her car and left. And what if she was cheating on Sean? Sure, it was scummy, but it's not like there was a law against it. How would he know it was going on? If he did, and that was when he'd given Samantha the bruise, wouldn't she have stopped?

The doors opened with a light ding, and I stepped out onto the sixth floor. What was I doing? None of this made any sense. It was ridiculous. I was being ridiculous. I stood in front of the elevator bank for about two minutes, thinking about my different options. Finally, I decided that I wasn't going to do anything about this. If Samantha *was* cheating on Sean, that was her business. It might have had nothing to do with the bruises Olivia had seen.

Either way, Sean wouldn't be here, which meant there was no reason for me to be either. Samantha wasn't in any imminent danger. I was just being nosy.

I turned and mashed the button to go back down to the lobby level. I was overstepping. Besides, I had a dinner to go to, and it would be starting in just a couple minutes.

About fifteen seconds after I pressed the button, one of the elevator doors opened. I waited for a man inside to step out and entered after him, and as the doors were closing, I realized it was Sean.

My breath caught in my throat as adrenaline rushed through my body, tingles crawling up my spine like tarantulas. I shot my hand out in between the elevator doors to stop them from closing. What was Sean doing here? How had he found Samantha? What was he going to do when he saw her?

I had no idea what *I* was going to do, but I couldn't just sit around and do nothing. I had a feeling this was going to end badly, whatever happened, and there was no time to call the police or even security. Sean had just reached the door.

I stepped out of the elevator and followed him.

Luckily, the deep carpet dampened the sound of my footsteps.

Sean reached into his pocket and pulled out a balaclava, which he yanked over his head. He then grabbed a white key card from his pocket and pressed it against the scanner on the door. A green light appeared, and he entered the room.

How on earth had Sean gotten a key to this random man's hotel room? How did he even know Samantha was here? Did he follow her? Why was he wearing a mask?

Sean entered the room, and I quickly lunged forward, catching the door before it closed. I kept it open a fraction of an inch so I could listen to what was going on inside.

"What the hell?" a man's voice said.

"On the ground!" Sean shouted. "Get on the ground! Where's your wallet?"

Holy crap. This wasn't an angry-boyfriend situation at all. This was a robbery.

A million thoughts raced through my mind at once as I tried to figure out what to do. I had no plan. I hadn't seen this coming at all. Why was Sean robbing this guy? Was Samantha in on it? She had to be. How else would Sean have gotten a hotel room key?

Suddenly, it all clicked. Sean wasn't abusive. Sean and Samantha were working together to rob men in their hotel rooms. The bruises must have come from one of their previous heists gone wrong. I'd completely missed it.

"Get your watch off," Sean ordered. "And get me

your wallet. And laptop. And anything else you have in this room that's valuable. Come on, do it now."

"Okay, okay," the man's voice said, wavering. "Let me just get some clothes on, okay?"

"There's nothing there worth hiding from me anyway. Just get the money. Now."

There was the sound of a scramble. Sean had to have a weapon of some sort given the fear in the man's voice.

I could just leave. I could close the door, go back to the elevators, and head downstairs as if I hadn't seen anything. Or at the very least, I could call the police. No one would blame me. It was what anyone else who was a grown-ass adult and had their life figured out would do.

But then again, a normal adult probably wouldn't have been here in the first place. Good life decisions had never been my strong suit. And the thing was, I wanted answers. I wanted to know what was going on with Samantha and Sean, and I didn't want this guy to get robbed just because he picked up the wrong woman at a random bar. Sean was a criminal, and I was pretty sure Samantha was too.

And I just couldn't sit around and let them do it.

I pulled out my phone and sent Jake a quick text with the hotel name, room number, and the fact that there was a robbery going down. I didn't wait for a reply. I decided to use the element of surprise to my advantage.

I counted to three and burst through the door. Sean would be the guy with a weapon, so I focused on him first. It was a typical hotel room: bathroom on the right as I entered. A queen-sized bed took up the majority of the rest of the room. Sean stood in front of the bed, a weapon pointed at the man standing next to it. The victim tried to cover himself with a sheet while gathering his valuables.

Samantha had gotten her underwear back on and was busy slipping back into her dress. I had just enough time to notice her eyes widen and her face contort into an expression of surprise as I launched my body into her boyfriend like a linebacker on cocaine. I let out a yell at the last second just to unsettle Sean a little further.

"What the—?" he had time to exclaim before the force of my body slammed into his, knocking the air from his lungs as the two of us collapsed to the floor.

"Who the hell are you?" Samantha shouted.

I obviously didn't reply. I hit my head on the carpet on the way down, and as soon as we came to a stop, Sean reached out to punch me. I rolled away from the hit and kicked out at him, connecting with his knee.

He let out a yelp then reached out and grabbed something from the floor, which he pointed at me.

At the last second, I realized I recognized that yellow handle. It was a Taser.

Sean pressed his finger on the trigger, and the two prongs shot out toward me.

Why did this always have to happen to me?

Chapter 16

I flinched as I prepared myself to feel the horrible sensation of thousands of volts of electricity coursing through me, but they never came.

Instead, it felt like a jolt of static electricity passed through my body then stopped.

I looked up at Sean, who looked down at his Taser. It was only then that I realized it didn't look like any of the regular-issue ones I'd seen.

"Did you actually buy a generic version of a Taser?" I asked with a grin. "Let me guess, you saw an ad on Facebook that totally looked like the real thing."

Sean looked at the no-name stun gun, pressing the trigger again and again. "The website said thousands of volts of electricity."

"Well, if you saw it on the internet, it must be true," I said. I ripped the prongs from my shirt and launched myself at him once more. Sean easily had eight inches and fifty pounds on me. I was going to need a miracle if I was going to beat him in a fight, so I figured throwing my entire body at his and hoping for the best was the way to go.

However, it quickly became obvious that that wasn't going to work, especially when Samantha was added to the mix. She grabbed the lamp from the bedside table and hurled it toward me. Luckily, I spotted it out of the corner of my eye at the last second and was able to duck out of the way. It smashed against Sean's arm, but it changed my trajectory enough that he was able to grab me by the hair.

I let out a yelp and kicked at him, but he threw me to the floor. I hit the ground with a thud, the skin of my arms burning as they rubbed against the carpet. He came toward me, but I swung out my legs and managed to trip him, causing him to fall next to me.

"You go, stranger!" the man whose room this was called out to me, while Sean grunted with a mixture of surprise and displeasure.

I needed an advantage. My eyes darted around the room and landed on the minibar. It was right next to me.

I stood up, feeling a little bit woozy, and Sean did the same. Samantha was pressed against the wall in the corner, looking as if she wanted to join in but was just too terrified to do so.

That was fine with me. I could barely handle this one guy, let alone two people.

I spun around and opened the minibar. I grabbed a bag of peanut M&Ms, ripped it open, and launched it at Sean's face.

"What the hell?" he said, holding his hands up in surprise.

That gave me enough time to grab a miniature champagne bottle, and in a single motion, I swung it around and hit him on the side of the head with it.

The bottle burst into a thousand pieces, shards of glass falling to the floor as the sweet, bubbly liquid exploded all over the room.

Samantha let out a scream as Sean's eyes rolled to the back of his head for a moment, and he fell to the floor, unconscious.

"Congratulations. That'll be thirty-two dollars, please," I said over his collapsed body, grinning to myself as I held the neck of the small champagne bottle. I'd totally just kicked his ass.

But I wasn't finished yet. I looked up and locked eyes with Samantha, who was still cowering against the wall. She let out a small squeak when she saw me then darted for the door. I sprinted after her, chasing her down the hall. Eventually, I dove for her, wrapping my arms around her legs and squeezing my eyes shut as the two of us fell together. My head slammed against her calves, and we came to a stop just in time for the elevator doors in front of us to open.

I looked up to see Jake standing there.

"This might be the first time in my life I'm actually glad to see you," I said.

"The first time, huh? Do you not remember literally yesterday?"

"Okay, second time. Samantha, you're under arrest," I announced as I scrambled back up to my feet.

Samantha let out a groan, obviously having given up.

"You don't get to say that to people," Jake said, shooting me an exasperated look as he pulled a pair of handcuffs from his pocket.

"Well, she *is* under arrest."

"Yes, and *I'm* the one arresting her. Not you. Now, get up," Jake said, hoisting Samantha to her feet.

"What are you arresting me for?" Samantha complained. "I didn't do anything."

"Assault, for one. We'll sort out the rest of the charges later."

"She's the one who assaulted me," Samantha screeched. She glared at me as Jake forced her arms behind her back and clipped the handcuffs on her wrists. "Why aren't you arresting her?"

"Because I'm obviously innocent," I replied with a smug smile. "You're the one who tried to rob the guy in that room over there. So, tell me, how does it go? You show up at the bar, you find a guy who's here by himself, maybe for a conference. He's got a wife, but she's back in Des Moines, so how will she ever know what he's doing? You start flirting with him, then you go up to his room. Somewhere along the line, you figure out how to get Sean a key to his room. Maybe you text Sean his name and room number, and he goes to the front desk to get an extra key.

"Anyway, you go up with him, and Sean follows you. The two of you start getting frisky, then Sean comes in and threatens him with the fake Taser. He immediately gives up his cash, and the two of you take off. He's too embarrassed and too afraid of his wife finding out what he did, so he doesn't tell anyone. Doesn't report it to the cops. The two of you get away with it. Until now. Do I have it about right?"

Samantha hissed in my direction as if she was an angry cat. "You've got it all wrong. You're not going to get any proof of any of that. It's just a story you made up."

"Oh, please," I said with a laugh. "You really think that guy in there isn't going to tell the truth? He's going to expose you for the fraud you are."

"That's right, honey," the man said, coming out of the room, still doing up his belt.

I finally got a good look at him for the first time. He was about five foot ten, in his early fifties, with only a couple whisps of white hair on the top of his head. He had on a white T-shirt that didn't hide the pudge from the seventy or so extra pounds he wore around his middle over a pair of black shorts. "There's been so much damage done to this room I need a police report so that I don't get charged for it. I told her I had a wife, and it's true. But she also died two years ago. There's no one out there who's going to be mad at me for cheating on them."

Samantha gaped at the man. "You told me you were married!"

"I still consider myself to be. I'm not moving on from Maria. She's still my wife, and she will be until the day I die. But I know she would want me to have my… needs… met. And then you and your boyfriend in there robbed me!"

"You deserve it, you know. You men. Honestly, how dumb can you be?" Samantha snapped. "You're a two out of ten, tops. How can someone like you possibly believe that I'd be interested in… that?" Samantha snapped, looking him up and down.

"Well, I'm sure you'll find someone suitable in prison," the man shot back at her.

"You might want to go in there and arrest her boyfriend too," I said to Jake. "I knocked him out pretty good with the champagne bottle, but I'm not sure how long it'll take before he comes to."

"Liam should be here any second now," Jake said.

Right on cue, the elevator doors popped open, and Jake's older, pudgier, and far dumber partner walked out.

"Other one's in the bedroom," Jake told him.

"On it. Why am I not surprised to see this one here?" he said, jerking a thumb in my direction.

"It's all right. I'm surprised to see you here too, doing actual policework," I shot back at him.

"I'll have you arrested for assaulting an officer," Liam snarled.

"I'd love to hear you explain to a judge how my words made you feel sad inside, and you felt it appropriate to arrest someone for calling you lazy," I replied.

"Okay, both of you, ignore each other," Jake said. "Liam, go into room 614 and arrest the man who's unconscious in there. Find out if he'll wake up himself or if we need to call a bus."

"I swear, if Sean is hurt, I'm going to sue the crap out of you," Samantha spat in my direction.

"That's enough out of you, too," Jake said to Samantha. "You're under arrest, and I'm taking you down to the station. Charlie, please tell me that's all the police presence you're going to need tonight."

"I sure hope so. To be fair, I had no idea this was going to go down."

"I actually believe you. I'm going to need a statement, but I can take it tomorrow."

"Copy that. I have to get back to the rehearsal dinner for the wedding anyway."

"You're just going to let her go? She attacked Sean," Samantha was shouting as I walked back to the elevators.

I gave myself a quick once-over in the elevator, decided that I didn't look like I'd just come out the other end of a fight with a robber, and walked back to the restaurant as if nothing had happened.

Luckily, I'd only missed the first couple minutes of dinner. Servers were still efficiently striding between tables, bringing over bowls of gazpacho. I slipped into my chair at one of the tables at the front, next to Heather, mumbling my apologies as I sat down.

"I'm glad you're here," Heather said, patting my hand reassuringly. "I want you to meet my two sons, David and John. And their spouses, Jennifer and Hugh."

I shook hands with the rest of Heather's immediate family. David and John, both in their mid-forties, were very obviously brothers and very obviously Heather's children. They all shared the same keen eyes that glimmered with excitement, the same noses, and the same thin mouth. David's hair was flecked with a little bit more gray than Hugh's, and his chin was stronger, but they were unquestionably related.

Jennifer looked uncannily like Miranda from *Sex and the City.* It wasn't just the red pixie cut and blue eyes, but she had the same face shape, slim figure, and small button nose. Hugh was square jawed, with chestnut brown hair that he styled to add an extra two inches to his height, wearing a pair of thick, round glasses, and when he introduced himself, he had a posh English accent, sounding as though he'd just returned from lunch at Buckingham Palace.

"Thank you for helping our mother," David said after I'd been introduced to the rest of the family. "We really appreciate it. It's such a difficult time for all of us. I can't imagine what Melissa is feeling right now."

He glanced toward the table at the front, where the bride and groom were seated along with the rest of the wedding party.

"She's handling it so well," Jennifer said, shaking her head. "I'm just so impressed by her. She's always been mature for her age, but this is something else. To have her father murdered like that, just days before her wedding, and not call it off. I don't think I would have been able to do it if it were me. I just don't."

"I just hope she's doing this for her and not for the rest of us," John said. "I'm certain everyone would understand if the wedding was called off temporarily, and anyone who didn't wouldn't deserve to get to celebrate the love between Melissa and Chet anyway."

"I'm quite certain she is," Heather replied.

"Good," John said. "I'm glad to hear it. And I hope Dad's killer is found. Unfortunately, I don't hold out too much hope for that happening, especially if it was simply a random attack. I'm sure those two FBI agents are doing their best, but they say the first forty-eight hours of an investigation are the most important. How are we supposed to know if they've gotten anywhere?"

"We don't, and that's by design. But they'll tell you if they find the person who did this. And speaking of, I believe that's them by the door," his husband replied.

I looked over my shoulder to the entrance. Sure enough, agents Forrester and Sparks were walking through the upper level of the restaurant, directly toward us.

"Do they have no sense of decorum?" David muttered under his breath.

"Hello, we're sorry for interrupting this dinner," Agent Forrester said. He at least had the decency to look suitably embarrassed for being here right now.

"Please, grab yourselves a couple of chairs," Heather said, motioning for the server, ever the perfect hostess. "You must at least sit down, even if it's only for a few minutes. We're so grateful to you both for the investigation. How are things going?"

A couple of the servers immediately returned with chairs, and everyone at the table shifted to make room for the new arrivals. Given the almost imperceptible look that passed between David and John, I knew neither one of them was especially pleased to see the agents here, during this dinner, but Heather was going to play the role of the gracious hostess all the same.

"The investigation is going well, and we do have some leads we're following," Agent Forrester said, looking around the table. His eyes landed on me and paused. "Have we been introduced? You look familiar somehow."

"Charlotte Gibson," I replied. "You probably know my face from the papers; I was involved in the Marion Hennessey murder case a few months back."

"Right, that must be it," Agent Sparks said, nodding.

The knot that had formed in my stomach unclenched. The last thing I needed was for these two agents to recognize me from the chase down the staircase earlier.

"What updates do you have for us on our father's murder?" David asked somewhat impatiently.

"I'm afraid we're unable to keep you up-to-date on exactly what process we're following," Agent Sparks replied.

"That's code for they don't have anything," David whispered loudly in his wife's ear.

"David," Heather hissed at her son.

"What, Mom? It's true. If they had arrested anyone, they would tell us."

"It's true, we haven't made any arrests yet. However, we're following up on some promising leads. Now, did any of you see Rex that morning?" Agent Forrester asked, looking around the table.

He was met by shakes of the head and blank stares.

"All right, now, what if I told you one of you was seen in the lobby that morning, speaking with him?"

I looked around the table, but again, there were only blank faces.

"John?" Agent Sparks finally asked. "Did you see your father that morning?"

"Me? What? No, I didn't, and anyone who told you I did is a damned liar."

"Are you sure?" Agent Sparks said.

"John was with me in our hotel room that entire morning," Hugh said, placing a protective hand on his husband's arm. "He couldn't have left the room before we were told of Rex's murder."

"Well, that's funny, because you told us you came down to the lobby around seven to get a latte from the coffee shop," Agent Forrester said.

Hugh's face flushed angrily. "Yes, but I was only gone five minutes."

"Five minutes during which your husband could have left the room and gone to speak with his father. Tell us, John, what was the topic the two of you spoke about?"

"There was no conversation, because I didn't leave the room," John snapped. "I don't know who fed you this load of bull, but that's all it is. Would that I had spoken to my father that morning. We could have had a nice conversation. One last memory before his passing. But it didn't happen. Who told you that it did?"

"I'm afraid we're not at liberty to share that information," Agent Sparks said.

"Oh, then you're just fishing," Hugh snapped. "Let me guess: nobody actually *told* you this information. You just thought you'd come in here, accuse my husband of something that didn't happen, and then see how we all reacted. Well, I for one am not having any of this. I will not allow my husband to be treated like a common criminal in front of his family."

"Out of curiosity," John said, leaning forward, "what motive do you have for thinking I could have done this to my father?"

"We're not saying you did," Agent Forrester said, holding up his hands. "We're just trying to gather as much information about your father's movements as possible from that morning. You're saying you didn't meet him on the path outside the hotel, near the bar he had visited before his murder?"

"That's correct. I didn't see my father that morning."

"Did you leave your room at all?"

"No."

"What about you, David?" Agent Sparks asked. "Did you leave your room that morning?"

"Yes. I went down to the beach to walk along the sand. But I didn't see my father there. I didn't see him at all."

"What time was that?"

"A little after six. I like to sit on the beach and watch the sun rise. I realize we're facing the wrong way to see it in the morning, but the colors are nice all the same."

"So neither one of you saw your father that morning?" Agent Forrester asked.

"No. Whoever told you that must have been mistaken," John said.

"Did you ever see your father with anyone you didn't know?"

"Plenty of times," John answered. "He was a real estate developer in New York, and I'm an engineer living in London. Whenever I saw my father, he was with someone I didn't know."

"What about here on the island?"

"No," John said. "I never saw him with anyone who wasn't part of the wedding party."

The others all agreed with that statement.

"Why were you brought in?" I finally asked. This was a good chance to get some answers for myself. "After all, couldn't the Maui PD handle this? Isn't that what would normally happen with a murder investigation?"

"There are certain instances in which the FBI is called in to investigate," Agent Forrester replied. "This is one of those cases."

"Sure. I get that. Stuff that has to do with kidnapping across state lines, that sort of thing. But none of that applies to this case. Rex Thunder was just an ordinary New Yorker, here on vacation, murdered by someone on the path just outside of the hotel where he was staying. What reason could the feds possibly have for investigating?"

"That's confidential information," Agent Forrester said, his tone frostier than the ice water in front of me.

"No, Charlotte is right," David said. "Why *are* you investigating? It's not just that Dad was rich. Lots of rich people get murdered, and they still just let the police investigate. What do you know?"

"All right. That's all we had to ask, so we'll leave you to your dinner," Agent Forrester said. "We'll be in touch if we have any news to share. We're not answering any questions about this investigation."

"And, um, enjoy the big day tomorrow," Agent Sparks added as the two of them rose from their seats and left.

Chapter 17

"I cannot *believe* the gall they had to come here during the rehearsal dinner and accuse me of speaking with Dad the morning he died," John hissed angrily when the two of them left. "It's unbelievable."

"We should complain to the field office chief," Hugh agreed. "It shows a total lack of decency."

I stayed quiet, eating my soup slowly as I thought about what had transpired. Had the agents just made it up? Were they goading the two men into trying to admit they had seen their father that morning? Had David actually seen Rex? Had he had a reason to kill him?

Deep down, I had to admit, I doubted it. I hadn't learned anything about these two sons to implicate them at all. And John appeared genuinely surprised at being questioned.

"I really want to know why the feds are investigating," John said. "They wouldn't tell us anything, and that's very telling."

"Could they believe your father was involved in something illegal?" Hugh suggested. "I know he would never, but he was involved in real estate, an industry known for its role in money laundering. Perhaps the FBI erroneously believe that his death was related to one of his business deals."

I kept my eyes carefully on my soup as I listened in on the rest of the conversation.

"I suppose that's possible," David said slowly. "But Dad was always very conscientious about doing the right thing. He'd never have been involved in money laundering."

"No, I don't believe he would have either. But it's all about what the FBI believes, isn't it?"

I knew Rosie was right. If the FBI believed Rex to be involved in some sort of illegal operation, they—or more likely, the CIA—had known about it *before* he was murdered. The question was: how were they involved? I was going to try and get some answers.

"Excuse me, I have to go to the bathroom," I muttered. I slipped from my chair and headed back to the stairs leading down to the main restaurant as quickly as I could without drawing attention to myself.

The two FBI agents were walking briskly through the lobby.

"Agent Forrester," I called out, and they both stopped. "Agent Forrester and Agent Sparks. I need to ask you something."

"You. You're the woman who was involved in the

Marion Hennessey thing," Agent Sparks said. "But I don't think that's where we know you from. How are you related to the family?"

"I'm not; I've been hired by Heather Thunder to help her through this difficult time."

"Where were you earlier today, around four?" Agent Forrester asked.

Whoops. It looked as if my wig and sunglasses hadn't been *that* good a disguise.

"At a friend's house in Kihei. But I didn't come here to talk about me. I want to know why you're investigating and not the local police, and don't give me that crap about how you can't say anything. There is a reason, and I think I know it: Rex was working for you, wasn't he? Or some sort of intelligence agency. Either way, Rex was doing something for the United States government, which is why you're on this."

Agent Forrester's face was impassive, but Agent Sparks looked over at his partner, his brow creased in worry, and I knew I was right. I'd gotten my answer.

"You're completely off base," the former replied.

I grinned. "Too bad your partner's face has given it all away."

Agent Forrester turned to Agent Sparks, looking at him as if he was a toddler who'd just had an accident in the middle of the floor. "You really need to learn to lie better."

Agent Sparks shrugged. "She obviously knew what she was talking about. What's the harm?"

"You know damn well the harm comes from civilians learning about our cases. Especially one like this."

"Since that horse has long since bolted, how about you tell me exactly what's going on then?" I suggested. "Rex was working for you. And by you, I mean the US government. What was he doing?"

Agent Sparks decided to compensate for his earlier gaffe by playing the tough guy, crossing his arms and resting them on his ample beer belly. "We're not going to tell you anything. This information is classified, and you're just a civilian."

"Please, stop trying to make up for it. You messed up, and I know the truth, so you might as well tell me what I want to know."

"No," Agent Forrester replied. "We can't tell you anything. It's classified. Why do you want to know, anyway? If you've just been hired to help Heather through this time, you shouldn't care what happened to her husband. You should just be worried about her. Leave the investigating to the professionals."

I really, desperately wanted to tell him that a real professional would have found the USB thumb drive hidden behind the fake outlet in Rex's hotel room, but that would have earned me a one-way express ticket to an interrogation cell, so for once in my life, I kept my mouth shut.

Well, mostly.

"Professionals?" I snorted. "Please. It's been two days, and you're nowhere. You had to try and ambush the family with a lie in an attempt to give one of you something to go off, because you obviously have nothing."

"It's not like you have anything more than we do,"

Agent Sparks snapped. "And you're not even supposed to be working this case. So get out of here before we arrest you for interfering with a federal investigation."

"Or worse," Agent Forrester replied.

I gave the two agents one last look before turning back and returning the way I had come. Sure, I hadn't gotten all the information I wanted, but I'd gotten enough. Rex had been working for the US government *before* he died. That was why the feds had been on this case from the start. It wasn't that they knew he was doing something shady for himself, they knew he was doing something shady because he was doing it for them.

That suddenly opened up a new motive.

I RETURNED TO THE TABLE AND FINISHED DINNER with the Thunder family. When the tables had been cleared and the guests began slowly making their way toward the exit, Heather held me back.

"You've found something, I can tell."

"I think so. A solid motive. Rex was working for the US government. Probably the CIA, but it could have just been the FBI, I guess. Either way, it was an agency with enough clout that they sent in the feds as soon as he was murdered. That's why they're investigating. They weren't on Rex's trail because he was dealing in something illicit. He was working as a spy *for* the American government."

Heather let out a deep sigh. "I suppose that's better

than doing it entirely for profit. But my goodness. Rex just couldn't leave well enough alone, could he? Was it really that hard to live an ordinary life in America without attracting any attention to ourselves? Thank you for telling me, at least. I only hope he never told the government about his past. I'll always wonder if they know."

"On the bright side, if they know, they don't seem to care," I replied.

"There is that. Well, I am glad you are making progress on my husband's case. I need to know who killed him. Thank you for coming tonight."

"Of course. Good luck tomorrow with the wedding. I'm sure it will be beautiful."

"Oh, yes. Apparently, there is a second photographer coming from a magazine to take photos to be sold to the *Post*, or so Melissa hopes."

"And what do you hope?"

"That Melissa is doing this for herself and not for anyone else."

"Me too."

I left Heather and was tempted to send Dot a quick text, but as soon as I sat down in Queenie's front seat, I was hit with a wave of exhaustion, as if every last ounce of energy I had left was being completely sapped from my body.

Apparently, I needed to get a bit of sleep before I was going to be in any shape to do anything else.

"All right, all right," I muttered to myself. "You win; we'll go to bed."

I started the car, blinked quickly a few times to wake myself up, and started the drive back to Kihei.

When I walked through the door, Zoe was at the dining table, drinking a smoothie and eating an apple while reading some sort of textbook. She looked up at me and let out a wolf whistle.

"You're looking nice."

"As much as I'd like to tell you if you play your cards right, you could get some of this, I'm actually way too tired."

"Wow, shot down by my own best friend."

"How do you still look fresh as a daisy? We've both been up since way-too-early o'clock, and while I feel like I got hit by a bus that slammed me into a tree that then fell on top of me, you look like you've just had a nice shower after a relaxing eight hours of sleep."

Zoe laughed. "I'm just used to it by now. My body has become accustomed to the idea that we're never going to get to sleep on a regular schedule ever again, and now it's had years of practice. Besides, you don't look that bad."

"I feel that bad. How was work?"

"Oh, never a dull day in the ER. We had one guy brought in by his friends. He was high on meth and they were worried about him. He figured he'd try to escape by climbing through the ceiling, which he did. Only he fell through one of the tiles and crashed onto the floor, breaking his leg in the process."

"Yikes."

"Then another woman came in with a variety of

symptoms; turns out she was pregnant. She then told me, and I'm dead serious, that she can't be pregnant because she put red Skittles *up there* before having sex, and that's supposed to stop you from getting impregnated."

"No," I said, gasping. "Red Skittles?"

"Only that specific color, apparently. So I gave her some antibiotics and a much-needed lesson in anatomy."

"I'm genuinely curious as to where she heard that."

"She told me, 'Everyone knows that.' So I'm not sure."

"Who knew I could have skipped all the pain from the IUD if I'd only known about the magic power of Skittles."

"Don't you start, especially now that you're actually getting close to a relationship soon. Speaking of, have you abandoned your plan to fly to Arizona and start a new life?"

I scrunched up my face. "Yes. I saw Jake today, actually. And it wasn't the most awkward thing ever, but mainly because I needed him to arrest me so that he could hide me from the FBI."

"And here I thought I was going to be the one with the weirdest stories today, but no, you came in swinging. Did they arrest you?"

"No. Jake managed to get me away from them. Although he did tell them I was being arrested on twelve counts of public urination and three counts of indecent exposure."

Zoe snorted, spilling a bit of smoothie onto the table. "Amazing. You're truly perfect for each other."

I scowled. "We are not."

"Did you actually talk about what happened like a pair of real grown-ups?"

"No. I figured not being arrested was more important."

"I guess I actually can't argue with that logic. I'm glad you weren't taken in."

"Me too."

"What did they want you for?"

"Breaking into a sealed hotel room. But I got what I needed. Rex had a thumb drive full of infrastructure information that he's selling. And he was working for the government. That's why the feds are in on it. I think it was some sort of sting. But I can't think straight right now. I'll sort it all out tomorrow after I've gotten a bit of shut-eye."

"Good plan. I'm going to do the same soon."

Before going to sleep, I sent Dot a text. *Got some information on Rex. He was working with the US government. I guess as some sort of undercover thing. I'll come by in the morning.*

I curled up on the bed with Coco in my arms and was asleep before her reply came through two minutes later.

Chapter 18

I woke up the next morning to the sounds of the birds chirping at the sun outside. When I rolled over, Coco grumbled at me for interrupting her rest, and then I got up and trudged to the kitchen, checking my phone. Dot had replied last night saying to come by whenever, so I put some food out for Coco, for when her hunger eventually dominated her will to sleep for fourteen hours a day, decided I could grab some coffee on the way, and headed out to Dot's place.

Rosie answered the door and ushered me inside.

"I hear you've gotten some more information on Rex's dealings," she said.

"Yeah, spill," Dot ordered, spinning around in her computer chair to face me. "Rex was working for the US government?"

"I don't have any hard proof, but going by Agent Sparks's reaction last night, I know it's true." I recounted the events of the prior evening to Dot and Rosie, and when I was finished, Rosie pressed her lips together.

"On the bright side, my name has yet to come up in any of this. I'm thinking it's more likely it was just a coincidence that these events happened to transpire on Maui. On the other hand, I'll still be much more comfortable when we have all the answers."

"You're thinking the person trying to buy the plans from Rex is the killer," Dot said to me.

I nodded. "I do. That's what makes the most sense. And the FBI offers the motive. Rex was obviously working for some sort of government agency. I imagine whenever the deal went down, it was supposed to be some sort of sting operation. The buyer would get caught up in the net and suffer whatever fate the CIA deems necessary."

"That sounds likely," Rosie agreed. "Given the scope of this, I think the CIA is ultimately the agency Rex was working with. It also makes more sense given his history."

"Anyway, let's say the buyer suspects something was up. He finds out Rex is screwing him over and decides an appropriate reaction is to hit him with a blow to the back of the head."

"Does that make sense though?" Dot asked. "Wouldn't the government know who Rex was meeting with? They would have been able to arrest him immediately, since they would have known his identity. But now they're still investigating, days later."

"I don't think they knew who Rex was meeting," I

replied. "He obviously went to great lengths to keep things secret. The feds didn't know where that thumb drive was, either. So he wasn't telling them everything. Maybe they don't know who he was dealing with."

"That's possible," Rosie said. "It depends on how this all got organized. Did Rex find the buyer first and then go to the government? If so, then he would have had the leverage to do things that way. Also, keep in mind that whoever Rex is dealing with is unlikely to be the final buyer. If, say, some oil baron is trying to buy the data so that they can destabilize New York's energy grid to increase gas prices, they're not going to come here themselves. They're going to send a middleman to do it for them."

"Right. So we have to find that middleman. Dot, did you see anything else on that thumb drive that might indicate who Rex could have been meeting?"

"No. I had a solid look at it too. It was just the schematics for various infrastructure in the state of New York. How Rex got access to it, I have no idea. But it's not the sort of thing you want in the hands of the wrong person. There was nothing else on that drive, either. I thought maybe there would have been some sort of back door, a way to let someone in after the buyer had gotten it, but it was clean."

"Okay. So the buyer's information isn't on there. We're going to have to do this the old-fashioned way."

"Oh, good. I was hoping I'd finally be able to come off the bench," Rosie said.

"She was here all day yesterday, pacing like a lion trapped in a small enclosure," Dot said. "I swear, if I had access to a tranquilizer gun, I would have used it."

"I'm just not used to sitting back and letting other people do things while I hide like a frightened child," Rosie replied. "I realize why we did it. It was too dangerous for me to expose myself. But now, we don't have a choice. If we're going to find out who killed Rex, we need to draw out the buyer. And who better to do that than me?"

"I mean, I could always give it a shot," I offered.

"Not a chance. The buyer would immediately know who you are. You're openly working for Rex's widow, after all."

"And as much as I'd love to be a part of the action, I admit that I'm more useful behind the computer screen," Dot said. "Rosie's right. It has to be her. Besides, it's looking less and less likely that Rex came to Hawaii to involve her in any way. Between that and the fact that we'll have a new identity created for her, Rosie's secret should remain safe."

"And on top of that, I do want Rex's killer found," Rosie said quietly. "I know what we had was a long time ago, but he was a good man. Whoever did this to him should face justice."

"Problem is, how are we going to do this? We can't exactly go around the resort, hanging up posters reading "FOUND: USB THUMB DRIVE BELONGING TO FORMER SOVIET SPY. IF YOU'RE THE BAD GUY HE WAS SUPPOSED TO SELL IT TO, PLEASE CALL.""

Dot snorted. "I think we can be a little bit more

subtle than that. We're going to have to do this on the dark web. I'll come up with a story. Give me the day to come up with a full plan and hash it out. I have to create a realistic identity for Rosie too, complete with an online history."

"Will do. I work at ten anyway."

"I'll be in touch."

When I returned home, two large black SUVs were parked in the lot. Well, using the loosest possible definition of the word "parked." One of them was stopped perpendicular to the yellow lines, taking up three spaces. The other was on the other side of the lot, toward the building. The front wheels were up on the curb and had knocked over one of the planters filled with morning glories.

I briefly considered turning right back around and leaving. After all, if I was arrested now, I'd miss my shift at Aloha Ice Cream. And while Leslie was an understanding boss, I still didn't want to leave her in the lurch. And frankly, I was curious as to what the feds wanted too. Plus I figured this way, maybe I could get some information from them.

So I parked Queenie, entered the building, and went up to our floor, where the feds were standing at my door.

"Do you not have to pass a driver's test when they send you to Quantico?" I called down the hall as I walked toward them. "Or do you get bonus points for causing damage to innocent people's property?"

"Excuse me, but we're federal agents," Sparks said, turning toward me and puffing out his chest. "Show us some respect."

"I'll show you all the respect you showed that poor pot of flowers that had nothing to do with any crime. Why are you here anyway?"

"Charlotte Gibson, we want to ask you some questions about your relationship with Heather Thunder and about your actions and whereabouts yesterday afternoon," Forrester said. "Mind if we come inside?"

"Certainly do. But I'm more than happy to chat with you out here in the hall."

"All right, fine," Agent Forrester said. "You came to us last night and said you were hired by Heather to take care of her needs in this trying time. And yet, when we googled you last night, your name comes up as a private investigator multiple times. That was also the capacity in which Marion Hennessey had hired you, wasn't it?"

"Yes."

"Why didn't you tell us this before?"

"I did. I specifically told you that I was the woman involved in the Marion Hennessey case. Yes, I am normally a private investigator, but times are hard for everyone these days, and if somebody wants to hire me to help them out whenever it's needed for a few days, I'm happy to play that role as well. I'm not going to say no to a paycheck, especially since this job doesn't involve me staying up half the night, watching two strangers bumping uglies. It's not the kind of moon I like to see at two in the morning, but that's the job, isn't it?"

"So Heather Thunder hasn't hired you to find out who killed her husband?" Agent Forrester asked, narrowing his eyes at me. "Because here's the thing. We don't believe you."

"Really? Heather is a nice old lady whose husband died just days before her daughter's wedding. She needed support on short notice and thought someone who's observant, used to problem solving, and quick on their feet would be the best person suited for the job. I was the person who solved the murder of James MacMahon, another real estate mogul from New York City that her family knew, and so she called me."

"You haven't denied that you're looking for his killer."

"Okay, fine: I'm not looking for his killer."

"You told us yesterday you were with a friend yesterday. Who would that friend be?"

"It was me," a voice announced from down the hall. Vesper, my neighbor, was just coming up the stairs with a pack of groceries under her arm. "Don't they teach you how to park down there at FBI school, or do they consider it a bonus if you miss the road entirely?"

Both men whipped around to look at her. "Oh yeah? What time was that?" Agent Forrester asked.

I quickly held up four fingers on one hand.

"Let me see. Charlie must have come, around I don't know, around a quarter to four? Stayed for a little while. I'm not entirely sure how long. We had a few glasses of wine, you see," she said with a wink.

Damn, Vesper was good at this.

"Can you narrow that down a bit for us?" Agent Sparks asked.

I held up two fingers.

"If I have to, I'd say around two hours? Something along those lines, anyway. Why? What do you think Charlie did?"

"I'm afraid that's classified information, ma'am," Agent Forrester replied.

"Besides, whatever it is, I couldn't have done it," I said with a casual shrug. "I was here. Now, are we done?"

"Yes, I've got some ice cream in here I'd like to get into the freezer before it melts," Vesper said.

Before she had a chance to move, however, another door opened down the hall. Franny poked her head out, and as soon as her eyes landed on the two agents, they widened.

"Are you real FBI agents?" she asked.

Agent Forrester scowled in obvious annoyance, but Agent Sparks grinned at her. "We sure are, kiddo," he replied.

"Can I see your badge?" Franny asked, coming out into the hall.

"You sure can," Agent Sparks said, and Franny skipped down the hall excitedly while Vesper slipped into her apartment. He handed her a card. "Do you know how to tell if this is real?"

"It has to come in a billfold, with the badge on one

side and your identification card on the other. Also, a lot of the fakes just say FBI on the top, whereas a real one will say Federal Bureau of Investigation. And if I'm still worried about the identification, I should call the closest field office, which on Maui is Oahu, to check."

Agent Forrester looked taken aback, but Agent Sparks just laughed good-naturedly. I liked him a lot more than his partner. "That's right, wow. Someone sure taught you well, young lady. Where did you learn all that stuff?"

"The internet," Franny replied matter-of-factly.

Vesper came back out into the hallway a moment later. Her ice cream must have been safely stored in the freezer. "You're still here?" she said to the two agents. "I thought I made it clear that Charlie was here with me at the time in question."

Agent Forrester turned to me. "You're *sure* that you weren't in Ka'anapali at the time in question?"

"One hundred percent."

"That's funny, because someone who looked a whole lot like you but blond broke into Rex Thunder's hotel room that day."

"Wasn't me."

"Are you sure?" Agent Forrester asked, a patronizing lilt to his voice.

"Seeing as you just got an alibi from Vesper over here, yeah. And you should be too. It's not my fault you can't find the actual person you're after, so you're trying to pin it on me. But that's not how the law works, is it?"

"No, it's not," Franny chimed in.

"Thank you, Franny."

Agent Forrester scowled, while Agent Sparks offered Franny a small smile.

"All right, that's all we've got for now," Agent Forrester snapped. "But don't leave town, and remember, we can hit you with obstruction charges if you interfere with our investigation."

"I saw how you drive; the only thing you seem to be able to hit are pot plants," I called out after him.

Franny covered her mouth with her hands to hide a giggle, while Vesper grinned.

When the two men had entered the stairwell to head down to the main floor, she turned to me. "You all right?"

"Yes. Thanks for the alibi. I appreciate it."

"Anytime. Once at the airport, the cops thought I had some weed on me. They searched my bag and everything."

I raised my eyebrows. "Did they catch you?"

Vesper grinned. "Didn't think to check inside my leg. Always check the prosthetic leg. Amateurs."

I laughed.

Franny ran back down the hall and returned a moment later with a walkie-talkie.

"What's that?" I asked her.

"I put one of those pens that lets you listen in on conversations that my aunt bought me in Agent Sparks's jacket when he showed me his badge. I wanted to see if I could sneak one past a *real FBI agent*," Franny said, her eyes glimmering with the excitement only an eight-year-old could muster.

"Well, it worked," I said with a grin.

"Now we can hear what they're saying," Franny said, proudly holding up the walkie-talkie.

"What's the range on that thing?" I asked.

Franny shrugged. "Dunno."

"What were you going to do if you got caught bugging a law enforcement officer?" Vesper asked with a small smile.

"If there's one thing I've learned from being eight, it's that everyone believes you're completely innocent and is willing to let you go with a stern warning," Franny replied, more mature and perceptive than anyone her age had any right to be.

"Okay, I need that walkie-talkie," I said, rushing to my door. "I'm going to grab my new binoculars, and I need to follow those two agents to see what they know."

"I want to come with you," Franny said.

"Where's your dad?"

"At work. Aunt Sally is here to watch me, but she fell asleep."

I considered my options. While I had never worked as a babysitter, I figured "take a small child on a trip to spy on some FBI agents" probably wasn't on the list of acceptable ways to spend a morning. But on the other hand, Aunt Sally was sleeping, and surely *some* supervision had to be better than no supervision.

"Okay. Fine. Stay here for a second."

I ran into my apartment, scribbled out a note for Aunt Sally with my phone number and explaining that I was taking Franny out for ice cream, then returned. I placed the note on the kitchen island in Franny's apartment, and the two of us headed out.

"We have to be quick; we don't know where they went," I said.

The two of us rushed to Queenie. Franny strapped herself in in record time, and I peeled out of the lot, tires squealing, trying to follow the two FBI agents.

Chapter 19

When we reached the intersection, I scanned the road, but there was no sign of the two agents. They must have driven off already. Franny was playing with the walkie-talkie, and while I could make out their voices, they were far enough away by now that heavy static prevented me from making out the words they were saying.

"Think they're headed back to Ka'anapali?" I asked, turning right onto South Kihei Road. "That's probably our best bet."

"I'll keep my eyes open," Franny said, straining against the seat belt as she tried to look past the cars in front of us.

Eventually, the roads opened up, and I spotted the two SUVs turning onto the highway toward Ka'anapali. We were going in the right direction.

"There they are," I said.

Franny squealed excitedly. "What are we going to hear them say?" she asked. "Do you think we'll get to know something super secret?"

"I don't know," I replied.

"Why were they at our place, anyway?"

"They wanted an alibi from me. Someone did something bad, and they think I look like her. But it wasn't me," I lied.

"I'm glad you didn't get arrested," Franny said seriously.

"Me too."

We pulled up to the traffic lights leading to the Honoapi'ilani Highway. The agents were also stopped at the lights, and now we were close enough that we could hear the conversation between them on Franny's walkie-talkie.

"It still makes sense that she's the woman who broke into the hotel room," Agent Forrester's voice was saying.

"I agree, but she has an alibi."

"We asked her about her whereabouts last night. She could have had time to set something up with that neighbor."

"True. But I don't really think she's involved. I think this is a dead end. We should just let it go," Agent Sparks said. "We'll see what Lucy has for us."

"Who's Lucy?" Franny asked.

I shrugged. "Your guess is as good as mine, but I think we're going to find out."

Sure enough, the two agents soon pulled off into

the parking lot at Olowalu Beach. Luckily, Leoda's Pie House was right across the street, and I turned into the lot, parking Queenie facing the road so we could look at the agents without being spotted. After all, we were parked on the other side of the highway. I grabbed the binoculars from the center console and watched as the two agents exited the car.

"They're going toward that lady," Franny said.

The lady in question was the photographer from the dinner the night before. She wore a maxi dress and sandals and looked impatient as the agents approached her.

"Well?" she asked when they arrived, her voice crackling through the speaker. "What have you got for me? Any news on who Rex's source might have been?"

"Sorry," Agent Sparks said. "We haven't gotten any further."

"Okay, well, I just spent two hours shooting pictures of the most depressing sunrise wedding on the planet, featuring a groom who's more attracted to his own biceps than anything with a pair of breasts and a bride whose smile is inspired by thinking about the cheque she's going to get from *the Post* for the photos the second photographer took. I'm bored. Do you know what my last shoot before this was? Hiding in the mountains in the Khyber Pass, watching a certain wanted war criminal pass into Pakistan and taking the pictures to prove it. Today? I've taken ten thousand photos of a smiling couple who obviously can't stand each other, and I'm frankly hoping she tries to murder him with a broken champagne bottle, because at least that would make this damn thing a little interesting. And all this because Rex wouldn't tell me who the hell he was meeting before he went off and got his head bashed in."

Suddenly, it clicked. Melissa had told me she had her father had looked at the portfolios of different wedding photographers together. Rex must have convinced her to hire this woman who wasn't a photographer at all. She was a government agent, and probably Rex's contact here on Maui. After all, they'd be able to meet without generating any sort of suspicion that way.

"You can't always get what you want," Agent Forrester replied. "Look, we're doing our best. We wouldn't even have to be here if the agency had actually gotten that basic info off Rex before he died. Now we're stuck investigating this murder when we should have had a suspect who was easy to hunt down."

"Look, we didn't have much choice in the matter." I had seen enough TV to know that 'the agency' always referred to the CIA. That meant that was who this woman was working for. "It's all stupid anyway. I'm sure whoever did it took the next flight off the island to avoid being arrested. There's no point, and I've told my boss that."

"You never know, Lucy," Agent Sparks said. "Whoever he was buying from might *really* have wanted whatever Rex was selling. If he even had anything. We didn't turn up any information from his room. It's also possible whoever killed him took what he was selling off the body."

Lucy shook her head. "Not a chance. The meet was set up for this afternoon. He wouldn't have just bandied about with it beforehand. You're sure you have no idea who he was selling to?"

"No. We're completely stuck."

"Well, then I'm screwed. I get to go explain to my boss that we know there's someone out there trying to buy high-stakes infrastructural schematics, and we're never going to know who it is. This was supposed to be a slam dunk. I was going to use it to try and get my next promotion. But I guess that's not happening now. Thanks, guys."

"Hey, this is your fault. You can't blame us for not being able to fix up your mess after the fact. It's your guy who didn't give you all the information you wanted. Your guy who got himself murdered and you who had to bring us in to try and clean up your mess," Agent Forrester snapped at her.

"I want to see what's going on," Franny whined, and I handed her the binoculars. After all, listening into the conversation was the more important thing.

"I think we can both take some of the blame here. This didn't go exactly the way I wanted it to. Rex was a little bit more astute than I gave him credit for. We have to keep things on the down-low."

"Yeah, and we have people asking why we're involved in the first place. Look, there's no point in arguing. Just know that our update is we don't have an update. We had a lead we thought was promising, but it's not panning out. We're getting stonewalled by everyone from the local police to the freaking family."

A lump rose in my throat like a ping pong ball released from the bottom of a swimming pool. That was *me.* I was the promising lead. The agents must have thought that I'd broken into Rex's hotel room to find the thumb drive because I was the one who was supposed to buy it off him.

Well, I now had even more incentive to get to the bottom of this case.

"I have to get back to the wedding," Lucy said. "The family is going to think something is up, and I have to be professional. I cannot have my real identity revealed. I'll be in touch."

With that, she climbed into a ten-year-old black Toyota sedan and drove off, heading north. The two agents followed her a moment later.

"Was that lady a real spy?" Franny asked in a hushed voice, her eyes gleaming with excitement.

"Sure sounds like it."

"That's *so cool.* We just saw a spy talking to the FBI. This is the best day of my life."

At least Franny didn't seem the least bit bothered that she'd just heard a conversation about a murder.

"I'm glad you had fun. How about we go grab a couple of pies to go, and then we'll head home?"

Ten minutes later, the two of us were on the road again. Franny was stuffing her face with the chocolate macadamia nut pie I'd just bought her. Mine was in a box at her feet, along with an Olowalu lime pie for Zoe and another chocolate macadamia nut pie for Sally. After all, I figured that might help her forgive me for basically kidnapping her niece for an hour.

"I'm going to be way too excited to do my homework today," Franny announced through a bite of pie. "Thanks for letting me eat this in the car. Dad never lets me eat in his. He gets worried about the mess, even though I'm careful."

"That's one advantage of the convertible. The wind takes care of most of the mess for me," I said with a wink, and Franny giggled. "You need to do your homework though. Otherwise, I'll send that spy after you."

"It sounds like she has more important things to deal with than me. What do you think her code name is? Do you think she has one?"

"I imagine so. I have no idea what it could be though. What would your code name be, if you had one?"

"Fennec Fox," Franny replied without hesitation. This obviously wasn't the first time she'd considered this question. "It fits because of my name and because they have big ears that help them listen for prey. I also like to listen to people."

"Yes, I've noticed," I said with a wry smile. I was going to have to be extra careful about what I said when I was near Franny these days, because who knew what kind of bugs she'd been planting on me?

"What about you? What would your code name be?"

"You know, I've never thought about it before."

"Really? That's weird. Well, let me choose one for you. Your code name should be Chipmunk."

"Chipmunk? Okay, I like it. Thanks, Fennec Fox."

Franny beamed with pleasure at having been referred to by her nickname of choice, and I drove her home, glad that this morning's excursion hadn't scarred her for life.

After a few hours of serving ice cream, I headed back to Dot's place, hoping she had a plan. After all, if the FBI agents thought there was any chance that I could have done this, I desperately needed to find the actual killer to clear my own name.

I walked in the door to find Rosie's appearance completely changed. She wore a chestnut-colored wig featuring beach waves that hung about six inches past her shoulder. Her makeup was mostly neutral but done in a way that made her lips look bigger, making her look like an older Julia Roberts. If I'd walked past her in the street, I wouldn't have recognized her.

"Wow," I said, admiring the look. "Who did this?"

"I did. One of the beauties of the internet is that there are a million video tutorials explaining how to make yourself look completely different using makeup. I used to be good at this back in the day, but thanks to YouTube, I'm now phenomenal."

"No kidding. So this morning, I found out some more information. The photographer at the wedding, which Rex found for Melissa, is actually his contact at the CIA. She met with the two feds who are investigating. And they actually think I'm the killer. I guess they believe that that's why I broke into the hotel room. So that's not great, but it's okay, because they can't prove it. And they didn't seem convinced anyway. They really have nothing to go on at all. They're lost."

"Good, that means they're not likely to get in our way," Dot said. "I spent the day planting some seeds on the dark web and got a hit. We found a buyer on the island who seemed *very* eager to get what was on this thumb drive. I purposely planned the meet within six hours so he wouldn't have time to fly out from the mainland if he wasn't already here."

"There can't be that many people in Hawaii browsing the dark web for that kind of information," I said, a grin spreading across my face.

"Exactly," Rosie agreed. "And even fewer willing to pay the seven-figure price tag Dot attached to it. That has to be the buyer and therefore the killer."

My phone binged just then, and I checked it. It was a text from Jake.

Are you around? I need to grab your statement from the other day. My boss is getting onto me about it.

"When is the meetup scheduled?" I asked.

"Seven-thirty, at the bar in the lobby of the resort," Dot said.

"Okay. I have to go see Jake and give him my statement from the other day. I'll come back when I'm finished."

"Is that what you kids are calling it these days?" Dot asked.

I glared at her. "Absolutely not."

"Sure, sure. Whatever you say."

The two ladies were chuckling as I left the apartment.

Chapter 20

Jake and I agreed to meet at Kamaole Beach Park II. I parked on the road and found Jake already sitting at one of the picnic tables under the large palm trees whose expansive network of fronds offered considerable shade. The sound of the ocean waves crashing against the shore masked the noise from South Kihei Road to the right as I sat down across from Jake.

"How's your case going?" he asked, tapping the yellow legal pad in front of him lightly with a pen. A soft breeze rustled his hair, and I tried not to think about how my hands running through it would have the same effect.

Nope. Definitely wasn't going to think about that.

"It's looking promising," I replied. "Actually, if you want to get one up on the feds, I can get you proof of who killed Rex Thunder tonight, hopefully."

Jake chuckled. "As much as I'd love to, it's their

case, not mine. So you should give whatever you've got to those two agents."

"They thought I did it. In fact, I believe there's a part of them that still thinks I did. Luckily, Vesper gave me an alibi, and it sounds like your captain gave them the runaround when they tried to find out who you arrested."

Jake grinned. "Yeah, that sounds about right. About fifteen years ago, my captain had a slam-dunk case taken from him by the feds, and he's still salty about it. He'll take any opportunity to screw over the FBI."

"Good. I'm not a big fan of being wanted by the FBI. I don't want my picture to end up on a top ten list that pops up on the TV at two in the morning in between infomercials. But it should all become moot tonight. We'll get the real killer."

"And you're going to stay safe doing it?" Jake asked, raising an eyebrow.

"Yeah. I'm not even going to be directly involved."

"I'm glad to hear it."

"How did your case against Samantha and Sean go, anyway?"

Jake chuckled. "You sure landed a good one in our lap. They've both lawyered up and are refusing to talk to us, but we got a search warrant and went through their apartment yesterday. We found evidence of at least eight different robberies, and we're trying to track down the victims now. So far, they all live on the mainland, and they're all married. None of them were particularly pleased to hear from us, so I don't think they're going to want to come back to the island to testify at a trial, but it probably won't be necessary. I think we've got enough on them to put them away for a long time without any more complaining witnesses. This isn't at all where I expected that case to go."

"Me either. I thought for sure Olivia was right and that Sean was abusive. But no, they were both working as criminals in tandem."

"I'm just hoping that once they serve their jail time, they're going to get the message and go back to the mainland."

"Me too."

"Anyway, why don't you run me through the whole story so I can get your official statement?"

I spent about twenty minutes telling Jake everything, and he scribbled down my story as we went. When we were finished, he had me date and sign the bottom, and I then slid the notepad back across to him. "There. Now you can charge them, or whatever. I'm willing to testify, obviously. That should add a few charges to the list."

"Thanks. Yeah, this case didn't quite go the way we thought, did it?"

"No. But then again, neither did that stakeout."

Great. I had to bring that up, didn't I? I couldn't just leave well enough alone and stay as far from that conversation as possible.

Jake cleared his throat. "Do you want to talk about it?"

"Nope." I focused on the breeze, wishing it would whisk me away to literally anywhere that wasn't this bench right now.

"Okay."

"It was a mistake."

Jake ran a hand through his hair. "Yeah. A mistake. It was late, and we were tired and wired on energy drinks and pizza."

"Exactly. We didn't know what we were doing. It happened, then it stopped, and we're going to pretend it didn't happen so I don't have to run away to Arizona and start a new life again."

"Arizona?" A small smile grew in the corner of his mouth.

I shrugged. "I decided I like the sun."

"Maui is better."

"It is," I agreed. "I want to stay here. Which means we have to stick to this agreement. We never talk about what happened again, ever. It was a mistake, and we repress it."

"Like healthy adults who know how to deal with our feelings and go to therapy regularly," Jake said with a chuckle.

I burst out laughing, knowing I sounded like a crazed banshee. "Yes. Exactly like that. Okay, good."

"Good."

"So that's settled then."

"We never have to talk about it again."

The two of us sat in awkward silence for a minute.

"Well, then," Jake finally said. "What else is going on in your life?"

"I followed the FBI with Franny this morning. We found out who Rex's CIA contact is. She's acting as the photographer for the daughter's wedding."

Jake raised his eyebrows. "You brought our neighbor's eight-year-old with you?"

"In my defense, she's the one who bugged the feds, not me. So she had the walkie-talkie. I couldn't just leave her there."

"Sometimes I genuinely wonder if you make up these stories just to see how I'll react, because there's literally no way any of that is true. And then I remember that I've actually witnessed you running away from the FBI after breaking into a guy's hotel room *this week*. I'm starting to understand how you ended up with a severed finger on your doorstep."

"Are you victim blaming me?" I asked, raising a single eyebrow skyward.

"I'd never dream of it. I'm just saying, you live an insane life. It's not your fault you attract the crazy. Mostly."

"If you're a part of my life, then you're part of the crazy."

"That is true. Okay, what's the weirdest thing that's ever happened to you that I don't know about?"

I thought about it for a minute and then grinned. "About ten years ago, I was walking back home from a party. It was probably nine in the morning. I might still have been more than just a little drunk. Anyway, it was a Sunday, so the streets were deserted. Then, all of a sudden, I was surrounded by people. I had no idea what was going on, but they were all running in one direction. I thought something had gone wrong, like there was an accident or something, so I started to follow them. Eventually, I realized they were running for fun. It was the famous Hot Chocolate Run that's held in Seattle every year. I was swept along, and before I knew it, I was at the finish line. Someone put a medal around my neck even though I didn't have a bib, and I got a mug of hot chocolate. I stumbled home, passed out, and woke up again about ten hours later. That medal is the only proof I have that I didn't hallucinate the whole thing. "

Jake laughed. "That's a good story, but I'm sure you have crazier."

"Okay, maybe. But you don't get to know them just yet. How about you? What's the weirdest thing that's ever happened to you?"

"Nothing even remotely close to that. My life is normal. Well, relatively normal, anyway. I've had some interesting things happen, but they haven't been weird."

"So what you're saying is that you're boring."

Jake smiled. "Yes, I'm boring. Compared to you, anyway."

"I'm going to take that as a compliment."

"It was meant as one."

The two of us sat in silence for a minute.

"I wish you were the one working this case," I finally said.

"Oh yeah? Why's that?"

"I trust you more than I trust those other idiots from the FBI. I mean, how bad of an agent do you have to be to let our eight-year-old neighbor plant a bug on you?"

Jake grinned. "If I remember right, she managed to do it to you too once."

"Yeah, but I'm literally completely untrained at this sort of thing. Besides, I eventually found it. Did she ever get you?"

Jake shook his head. "No. I don't think she's tried it on me, actually. I think her dad told her she's not allowed to use it on the honest-to-goodness cop that lives in our building."

"Yeah, that would make sense. She's a good kid. And a clever one."

"I wouldn't be surprised if that kid grows up to be president."

"Or Jason Bourne."

"Possibly that too."

"I mean it though. There's a lot at stake on this case, and I don't like that we're having to put our faith in the FBI."

"What's going on with this case? Why is it so important?"

I shook my head. "I can't really say. But it's important. It's more than just some random tourist getting murdered before his daughter's wedding."

"A lot of the time, murder cases end up more complicated than they appear at first glance. So do a lot of crimes, really. I mean, sure, sometimes you have crimes of opportunity or people making a mistake or doing something dumb because they were drunk or whatever. But once you move on past those to the crimes that were premeditated, thought out, things tend to get complicated. Because people are complicated."

"You're right. All of us have secrets that we don't tell random acquaintances, don't we? Someone passing me in the street would never know I moved here because a gangster left a finger on my doorstep after I killed his brother in a botched robbery. And that lady walking along the sidewalk right now could be a schoolteacher who makes penis-shaped cookies she sells on Etsy in her spare time, and she doesn't want her coworkers to find out about it for fear of losing her job. So she keeps it to herself. Hell, we spied on Samantha and Sean, thinking that he was abusive, when it turns out the two of them were running a racket to steal from tourists. It's all about digging down to find out who's keeping what as a secret and then working out a motive from there, isn't it?"

"Exactly. What secrets did your victim have? And more importantly, what secrets did the people around him have that could have resulted in his death? That's where you'll find your answer."

"Yeah. We've got a plan in place; we're going to find the killer. And then we have to prove it. We know the motive. We're just trying to figure out the who."

"Good. As long as you stay safe."

"It's all right. I've already been Tasered once during this investigation. I'll be fine," I said with a wink.

"You do realize there are very few people on the planet who need more than one hand to count how many times they've been Tasered, right?"

"Is that your way of telling me I'm special?"

Jake shook his head. "I just want you to be safe."

"I will be. I'll have Dot and Rosie with me tonight."

"Somehow, I don't feel like those two are the best possible influence."

"On the contrary."

"Okay. Well, listen, if you do get in over your head and you need help, text me. I can't guarantee I'll get there, since I'm working tonight, so I'll likely be in Kihei most of the evening, but if there's an emergency, let me know. I can make sure someone gets out there to you."

"Thanks. I appreciate it."

"Just try not to get yourself arrested, okay? I can't help you if you're in federal custody."

"I always do my best," I said with a cheeky smile. "Let me know how things go with Sean and Samantha."

"Sure will. It would be easier if they just gave it all up, especially since I think we actually do have enough evidence to convict, but some people just won't make a deal."

"They think they can get away with it. They're the kind of people who have done this for so long they think they're invincible. They believe they're smarter than everybody else, and it's going to come back and bite them."

"Definitely. Unfortunately, it also means more paperwork for me."

"Not a fan?"

"If I wanted to sit at a desk all day, I'd become an accountant."

I laughed. "Well, I'll leave you to it then. For what it's worth, I also would have made a terrible accountant. I've never been any good at math. I did like science though. As long as it was on land. Marine biology is creepy. Anyway, I'll see you later."

And with that, I slid off the bench and headed back to Queenie.

Instead of driving right back to Dot's place, I continued driving down South Kihei Road, absent-mindedly tapping my fingers on the steering wheel as I considered the words Jake had said. Something in my brain was trying to click, and I couldn't quite put my finger on what it was.

It all came down to motive. Everyone had secrets, and it was all about figuring out what someone's secret was.

In this case, who was the person hiding that they were acting as a buyer, probably a middleman, for some sensitive information that shouldn't be landing in the wrong hands? Or was I looking at it the wrong way? What if Rex was the one with the secret?

Then it clicked. He *was* the one with a secret, and it all went back to what the bartender had said that first morning. Rex had been in the bar a handful of times. But he'd only been on the island a couple of days at that point. Nobody goes to a bar "a handful of times" over the course of a day.

I spun the car around, tires squealing as I made a U-turn. I had to get back to Dot's place. I knew exactly who had killed Rex.

Chapter 21

I burst through the door of Dot's apartment as soon as Rosie answered it. "I know who Rex's killer is. I know who we're meeting tonight."

"Good," Dot said. "The more we know, the better. Who is it?"

"Alan, the manager of the resort. It all makes sense."

The two older women waited for me to continue, and I paced around the living room as I explained it all, trying to corral all the thoughts running through my head like a sheepdog herding a scattered flock.

"Okay. Let me think. So, the bartender that first day told us he had served Rex a handful of times. That's the key. A handful. Rex was murdered on Wednesday morning, but they had landed on the island Monday night. So realistically, the only time the bartender could have seen Rex was on Tuesday, but who goes to a bar a handful of different times in a single day? Nobody, that's who. If you're going to bar hop, you go to different bars. And I don't think Rex was that type. Are you with me?"

"Yes," Rosie said. "I agree. So that means…"

"That this wasn't Rex's first trip to Maui," I interrupted. After all, I was on a roll. "Everyone else has told us Rex had never been to the island before. He didn't know anyone here. And yet that's obviously incorrect. So why was he hiding the fact that he was coming here?"

"This isn't the first time he's sold illicit information to a buyer," Rosie said.

I pointed my finger in her direction. "Exactly. Heather obviously had her suspicions. She told me as much. She was worried Rex was involved in something like this, but it wasn't a new thing. This had been going on for a while. I'm not sure how long, exactly. But long enough that his wife noticed, although she reacted by burying her head in the sand as deeply as she could."

"Okay, I'm with you," Dot said. "But how do you know who his contact is?"

"The CIA agent, the one I saw earlier today chatting to the two feds on the case, she was the photographer. Rex recommended her to his daughter. I'm sure of it. You know what else he recommended? This hotel. Why would he do that? Because he specifically wanted to be there. And who does he know at the hotel? The manager. A man who has known Rex for years. Who worked at the same chain back in Manhattan. That's how Rex would have gotten into contact with him in the first place."

"Yes," Rosie said slowly. "That would make sense. He could have been selling information to Alan for years. Then, who knows? Perhaps he was found out on his last trip. Or perhaps Rex had simply had enough of what he was doing. He was either contacted by or got in contact with the right agency. Alan found out about it and killed Rex."

"I also believe Alan searched the hotel room. After all, he told me that he offered up his office to Heather so that she could speak to the police there in private. But I think when he did that, he went up to the room to see if he could find the thumb drive Rex had hidden. He still wanted the information. He probably has a boss somewhere out there who desperately wants that information."

"Okay. It all fits. So let's say you're right. Tonight, Rosie will be meeting him. We will have a full setup. Rosie will be wired up, and we'll record the entire conversation. As soon as Alan has the key, we can give the recording to the CIA agent and the feds, and they can sort out who gets him first between themselves," Dot explained.

"Are we actually going to give him the thumb drive?"

"We've been arguing about that for the last hour or so. I think we should give him something fake, but Rosie insists that he's going to check it at the bar if he's smart. And I think we all agree, Alan's not dumb."

"No. And this isn't his first rodeo either. I agree with Rosie," I said. "He's going to want to check the data before he sends the money. I think giving him something fake is too much of a risk. How is the transfer happening?"

"Bitcoin transfer," Rosie replied. "The go-to way to launder money or to perform otherwise shady transactions these days. No one is reporting a seven-figure wire transfer to the government when you're using cryptocurrency. We have the accounts already set up. We're prepared, as I'd expect the transfer will take place on location."

"Should have asked for more money if the two of you are getting paid," I said, raising an eyebrow.

"Oh, please. We're going to invest in TestosterZone," Dot said with a laugh. "That'll be a great way to see all the money go down the drain."

"More accurately, we'll be giving the wallet information to the government agencies," Rosie said. "They'll need it as evidence in their prosecution of Alan."

"I've told her that's boring, and the recording should be evidence aplenty, but *someone* doesn't want to technically be on the hook for selling state secrets," Dot said, rolling her eyes good-naturedly.

"Gee, I wonder why," I said. "Okay, it sounds like we're ready to go. Personally, I want to know who Alan is working for. There's no reason for him to want that information, since it would be useless to him. He's got to be the middleman. So who's he selling it on to?"

"If we're lucky, we'll find out," Dot replied.

The three of us piled into Rosie's CR-V—a little bit more subtle than Queenie—and drove up to Ka'anapali well in advance of Rosie's scheduled meeting with the mystery person I was ninety-nine percent sure would end up being Alan.

He was the murderer, and now we just had to prove it.

After Rosie had parked the car but before we exited, the three of us went over the plan once more. Dot would be in the lobby, manning a computer she'd brought. She would be recording the conversation, plugged into the hotel's security, and basically running point on anything else that was needed. Rosie, obviously, would be at the bar, waiting for Alan. And I would be hanging out nearby, pretending to be waiting for Heather while secretly taking video of the meeting as additional proof that Alan was the buyer—and the killer.

"I'm going to do my best to get him to admit to the murder straight up," Rosie announced. "I'd like as much evidence as possible."

"Careful though. You don't want to spook him," Dot said.

"No. I won't. But we have to prove that not only was he the buyer, he was the one who killed Rex."

"I think it's a good idea, and not only because I feel like I've got that particular sword of Damocles hanging over my head," I said. "The more evidence we get, the better. Ultimately, I was hired to find out who killed Rex. And to find out who knows what about Heather."

"How are you going on that side of things?" Rosie asked.

"So far, so good. I haven't heard a single peep from any members of law enforcement concerning Heather. I don't think anyone suspects her of being anything other than an innocent wife of a man who independently decided to get involved in some shady stuff and help the US government in the process."

"She'll be pleased to hear that, at least," Rosie said.

"I agree. But she'll be happier when Alan is locked up and all of this is behind her."

Before we reached the entrance to the hotel, the three of us split up. Dot entered first, computer in hand, headed to the lobby. About three or four minutes after that, I went through, playing with my phone. About a minute later, a call came through, and I answered.

"Can you hear me?" Dot asked.

"Sure can," I replied.

"Affirmative," Rosie said. Dot had given us all tiny earpieces that connected to our phones via Bluetooth, and we were all on a group call that would allow us not only to communicate with each other but also to hear anything Alan was saying to Rosie.

I headed toward the bar and leaned against the wall on the outside, playing with my phone, pretending to text like a good millennial. As far as anyone would be able to tell, I was waiting for somebody to come down and meet me.

About five minutes later, Rosie walked past me. She was brisk and efficient, motoring toward the bar and settling herself down at one of the tables in the far corner. She faced the entrance, so there was no way she could be surprised from behind.

This was it.

My heart thudded like a bass drum as I waited for Alan to show up. I kept finding my eyes flittering to the clock at the top of my phone, checking to see how long it would be before he should arrive.

They had agreed to meet at seven thirty. The lobby was bustling with people now. There were exhausted-looking tourists, returning to the hotel after having dinner off-premises, the long day of vacation activities behind them. There were the much more excited children bustling around, laughing and running, their feet slapping against the floor, the sound echoing through the open-air lobby. There were the more relaxed tourists, the ones who had spent the whole day either by the pool or on the beach, meandering through as they went to find somewhere to enjoy a late-night cocktail or a nice walk along the path. Staff members strode past as well, hustling to keep the hotel working like a well-oiled machine.

From the far end of the hotel, a bit of music pumped. That had to be the wedding reception in one of the ballrooms, where everyone was celebrating the new bride and groom.

Yes, it was busy here tonight. That likely suited Alan, but it suited us too. He wouldn't start a scene around this many people.

Minute after minute passed, however, and Alan didn't show up. Nobody did. Rosie sat at her table, sipping a drink. I glanced up at her from time to time. She never looked nervous, but I certainly was.

"He's fifteen minutes late," I finally muttered. "What's he waiting for?"

"Patience," Rosie said. "There are a million reasons he might not be here yet. He's likely staking out this whole place. He doesn't want to fall into a trap. Can you blame him?"

"Yes," I muttered sourly. I wanted him to show up so Rosie could ensnare him in her web and wrap him up in a nice little package for the feds.

"Dot, do you have the security footage?" Rosie asked.

"No. I'm having some trouble finding the access point. I don't know if they've changed things since the other day or what's going on. It should be fine; I don't think we'll need it, but I don't like this."

"Okay, well, I'm looking suspicious now, just hanging out at the bar forever," I said. "I'm going to head down to the wedding reception so it looks like I'm actually going to find Heather. Who knows, maybe he's waiting for me to leave before he approaches Rosie. If I hear the conversation between you starting, I'll come back."

"Be careful, Charlie," Rosie said quietly.

"I will."

I turned and went down the hall, following the sound of the music as I walked toward the main ballrooms. A growing feeling of unease rose inside of me, bubbling up like a boiling pot of pasta water that I'd forgotten to turn down.

Something was wrong. I didn't like this. I didn't like it at all. Why couldn't Dot get into the security camera footage like she always did? Why wasn't Alan meeting Rosie at the time he'd said he would? It had now been over fifteen minutes, closer to twenty, and nothing. Like, okay, I wasn't always the most punctual person on the planet. I was known to be late to appointments. But twenty minutes? And when I was paying seven figures for some information I wanted to sell on to some mysterious shadow figure?

No. That was the sort of thing you made an effort to show up on time for. No one ever kept James Bond waiting in a lobby.

Still, I passed into the hallway that led to the ballrooms. This was a huge hotel, and the hall was long, with numerous smaller conference rooms to the side. Farther down the hall were a couple of bathrooms and a bank of elevators. After that was the ballrooms, where the reception was taking place. With nearly three hundred attendees, the noise was getting louder here.

This was ridiculous.

"I don't like this," I finally said. "I don't like it at all. Is he here yet?"

"No," Rosie said. "I'm starting to agree with you. Dot, I dislike that you're unable to get into the security camera footage. This is normally something you're good at. What's going on? Do you think we've been compromised?"

"It's like they're just completely shut off," Dot said. "I can't find any sort of entry point."

"Okay," Rosie said. "I think we need to cancel.

Something is wrong. We meet back at the car, and we try this again another day. Dot, you leave first. Charlie, you're second. When the two of you are safe, I'll follow."

I was just getting ready to turn around and head back to the entrance when I felt a sharp sting in my neck, and everything went black.

Chapter 22

When my eyes fluttered open, I was lying facedown on the ground. I paused, taking a second to gather my wits about me and to observe the space. Nothing in my body hurt. That was a good sign. But when I tried to move my hands and feet, I found them bound. My hands were behind me, wrapped with duct tape. My feet were also bound.

Okay, that wasn't ideal. But at least nothing was broken or especially painful. Next, where was I? I was alone, obviously. Nobody had spoken when I moved a little. I was lying on a plastic sheet, and as I turned my head to the side, I saw a bed. On the other side was a media stand. I was in a hotel room.

Lying on a plastic sheet.

This did not bode well for my chances of survival.

Everything came flooding back to me then. We were supposed to be entrapping Alan, Rex's killer. He was supposed to meet Rosie at the bar, where she would sell him the thumb drive, but he'd never showed. We were going to bail, but I was attacked before I got the chance.

It wasn't a stretch to assume Alan was the one who had brought me here. It also wasn't a stretch to assume he was going to kill me whenever he got back from whatever he was doing. So I didn't have a lot of time.

I sat up as quickly as I could, and my head began to spin. Taking a moment to let it settle, I looked around the room. It was a standard hotel room. Bed, small table, TV stand, bathroom near the entrance. Coffee machine with complimentary tea and coffee. Minibar.

The most important thing right now was finding a way to free myself. My hands were tied behind my back, but at least they were free. Squirming around like a slug on cocaine, I cursed myself for not occasionally doing yoga while I tried to get up onto my knees.

Who knew doing that single sit-up last year wasn't enough to give me the core muscles of a professional athlete?

Luckily, adrenaline was a hell of a thing, and I eventually managed to struggle to my knees. Slowly shuffling on them toward the minibar, I opened it with my nose, only hitting my face on the corner of the fridge once, and for the second time this week, I grabbed a mini champagne bottle from the inside of the fridge. These were coming in handy.

This time, I smashed it against the side of the media stand. It took a couple of attempts, since with my hands tied, I had to twist my whole body with enough force to smash the bottle. But I got there, and I immediately began hacking away at the tape with the top of the mini champagne bottle. It was awkward work; the tape was thick, I couldn't see what I was doing, and a few times, I missed, piercing my ankle with the glass bottle.

Still, a bit of blood was better than being dead, which I knew would be the result if I was still here when Alan returned. After all, why else have the plastic sheeting on the ground? I'd seen enough mob movies to know that was there for one reason and one reason only.

Finally, with one last jab of the bottle into the duct tape, it snapped, releasing my legs so quickly I lost my balance and fell forward onto the plastic sheeting. Whatever. My legs were free, which gave me more freedom to figure out how I was going to get my hands loose.

On the other hand, now that I had legs, I could always leave the room. That was probably safest, after all. If I made it down to the lobby, I could call for help.

Yes, that was smarter than trying to get my hands free here.

I ran toward the door. After checking the peephole to make sure Alan wasn't immediately outside the door, waiting for me, I saw the coast was clear and opened it. I darted out into the hall, my hands still tied behind my back, and began running toward the elevators.

With a ding, one of the doors opened, and I stopped in my tracks when I found myself face-to face with Alan. His expression went from one of worry to one of surprise, and he raised his arm. That was when

I noticed the gun. There was a silencer attached to the end of the muzzle.

"Looks like I'm taking the stairs," I muttered, immediately turning and sprinting in the opposite direction. The gun popped, sounding like no more than a crushed can of soda being refilled with air, and a spot on the wall next to me exploded into splinters.

As it turns out, running with your hands duct-taped behind your back is not the easiest thing in the world to do. It reminded me of doing the three-legged-race with friends back when I was in preschool. I sort of half ducked my head in the hopes that if I got hit by a bullet, it wouldn't kill me.

Of course, getting nailed in the butt probably wouldn't be that fun either, and I would be mercilessly mocked forever by all my friends, but it was still better than being dead.

The gun popped another couple of times, and I squealed. I reached the thick fire door that led to the stairs, pressed myself against it, pushed it open, and immediately ran down the stairs.

I knew Alan was coming after me. There was no doubt about that. I also didn't have a clue what floor I was on or how close I was to the lobby. Luckily, when I reached the next landing, a giant 6 imprinted on the door told me exactly where I was. Six floors up was a long way, especially since I could hear Alan's footfalls on the stairs behind me.

I went down another level then grabbed the door leading to the fifth-floor hallway with my hands and awkwardly yanked it open. He was too fast; there was no way I was going to make it to the lobby, so I had to try and sneak away.

Or do something. Anything.

I launched myself down the hallway, heading toward the elevator. I didn't have a plan. I was just desperately running, trying to survive. But if I ran, I was just going to get caught, wasn't I? It was just a matter of time. No, I needed to go on the attack.

As soon as I reached the elevators, I mashed the down button as hard as I could. I heard the door at the end of the hall swing open; Alan was obviously coming after me.

The elevators were located in a small alcove in the center of the straight hallway, with staircases at either end. Right now, he wouldn't be able to see me.

To the right of the elevators were two vending machines, one for food and one for drinks, as well as the standard hotel ice machine. Nowhere to hide there. On the other side of the elevators was a simple side table, more like a stool, on which sat a handful of today's *New York Times*.

That wasn't going to be especially helpful either. I could have used the table to try and hit Alan over the head, but I'd need my hands to be able to do that.

Instead, I pressed myself flat against the wall, listening as I heard Alan's footsteps running toward me. As he got closer and closer, I timed my moment and stuck my foot out as he ran past.

I hit my target perfectly, and Alan pitched forward, the gun flying from his hand as he fell to the ground. I raced after the gun as it slid away, reached it, and kicked it even farther down the hall while Alan scrambled to his feet.

"Why won't you just lie down and die like a good little girl?" he snarled at me. His brow was covered in a sheen of sweat, and his suit was torn in a couple places. He was panting hard, and I figured now was a good chance to get the upper hand.

"I never was all that good at doing what I'm told," I replied, running toward him.

Because I had no hands, I must have looked like the world's most awkward ostrich running along. At the last second, I lowered my head to hit Alan in the chest. He let out an "oof" as the air exploded from his lungs, and the two of us collapsed together on the ground.

I was really getting tired of fighting dudes in this hotel's hallways.

I rolled awkwardly onto my side, and Alan immediately kicked at me. His toe connected with my shin, and I let out a yelp and rolled backward, doing the world's worst reverse somersault. I had never felt less athletic in my life.

Just then, the doors to the elevator opened. This was my chance. I threw myself into the metal box and slammed the button for the lobby as hard as I could with my hands still tied behind my back before mashing the "close door" button as if my life depended on it.

"Come on, come on," I muttered as the doors activated. They moved slowly, the mechanical equivalent of a *honu* trying to get to the other side of the beach. And just before the doors came together, Alan flew between them, landing inside with me.

Damn it. Another two seconds, and I'd have been free.

He grabbed me by the throat and pressed me against the wall. The back of my head smashed against the glass frame advertising the happy hour specials at the restaurant downstairs, and my vision blurred as I struggled to breathe.

If I didn't do something, I'd be dead before the elevator reached the lobby.

I kicked out, aiming directly for the balls. I made contact, and Alan howled with pain, the surprise causing him to let go of my neck. The doors opened then, and I shoved my way into another hotel hallway, past a family of four that gaped openly at me.

It looked as if the elevator was making one other stop on the way to the lobby.

Alan turned and lunged toward me again. We were on the second floor. In front of me was a waist-high barrier, behind which was a man-made river that created the waterfall leading down to the fountain in the lobby. I didn't really have a ton of options here. I reached the barrier, awkwardly tumbled over it, and was immediately taken by the current.

My head was immediately pulled underwater, and I had to resist the urge to inhale in panic. Everything was fine. My feet touched the bottom; the water up here on the second floor couldn't have been more than three feet deep. How deep was the pool at the bottom of this man-made waterfall, though? Hopefully deep enough. Surely I wasn't going to be the first person to be swept over. There had to have been more than one drunken accident in the history of this hotel.

I pushed upward with my feet, and my head broke the surface. I inhaled deeply, having just enough time to recognize I was going over the fall before my body was swept over. My stomach leapt into my throat as I tumbled freely for what felt like an eternity, but it was likely only a second or so before I landed in the fountain in the lobby with a splash.

A professional diver I was not; I landed on my back with a splat, sending water flying everywhere, but at least I didn't crack my head on the tiles below.

It took a moment for me to get my bearings. Sputtering, I emerged from the fountain like the creature that tried to drag Frodo into the depths of a lake in the first *Lord of the Rings* movie. I immediately looked up to see Alan staring down at me from the second floor.

"Charlie!"

I spun to see Rosie and Dot at the edge of the pool. I rushed over to them.

Rosie had a knife in her hand, and she immediately motioned for me to turn around. With a single slash, she undid the tape that bound my hands.

"He's there! We have to get him!" I said, motioning to Alan. "We can't let him get away."

The three of us ran to the elevator banks. One of the elevators had just stopped on the second floor, going up.

"He's going back to get his gun, on the sixth floor," I said.

"I'll take the stairs," Rosie said. "We have to seal off the exits. Dot, you take the other ones."

"Are you kidding?" Dot said. "I'll die of a heart attack if I have to run up six flights of stairs. I'm taking the elevator."

"I'll go," Heather said, appearing out of nowhere. "You take the north stairwell. I'll take the south."

Rosie nodded curtly, and the two of them ran off in opposite directions just as the elevator doors opened. Dot and I jumped in and immediately pressed the buttons for the sixth floor.

It felt as if the elevator was taking an hour to ascend. Calming Muzak emanated from the speakers, in stark contrast to the adrenaline running through my body.

"So, this hasn't gone exactly the way we'd planned it, huh?" Dot said as the metal box rose.

I couldn't help it; I burst out laughing. "Yeah, no kidding. He's going for his gun up there, so be careful when those doors open."

When the elevator reached the sixth floor, Dot and I pressed ourselves against the sides, but no hail of bullets came flying in. Alan was rushing down the hall toward the gun. I sprinted after him and launched myself onto his back.

I wasn't strong or heavy enough to cause him to fall, but Alan began spinning around, trying to get me off him. He slammed me against one of the walls, but there was nothing like the knowledge that if I were to let go, my life was likely over to keep me clutching onto him like the world's most aggressive leech.

I tried kicking and scratching, but then I heard Dot's voice. "Charlie, let go!"

I did as she ordered and immediately dropped off Alan's back. A shadow loomed over me, and I threw myself backward as the drink machine resting by the side of the elevator toppled over.

Alan had just enough time to let out an exclamation of surprise before the machine landed on him, crushing him.

One of his legs jutted out from under the machine at a weird angle, and a little bit of blood began pooling from his head onto the carpet.

"Rest in Pepsi," Dot cried out triumphantly.

Heather and Rosie appeared from opposite ends of the hall. They were both breathing heavily.

"Okay, if this was 1974, I would have gotten here before that elevator," Heather panted. "But I've learned my lesson. Next time, I'm not taking the stairs."

Rosie laughed hoarsely. "I'm with you."

"Is he dead?" I asked, looking down at Alan.

Rosie dropped to her knees and checked for a pulse. "No. He's alive. Security will be here in a minute. Get them to call an ambulance. Heather and I have to go. We can't be here when they arrive."

"Go," I said.

The two women shared a curt nod and immediately got up and ran back toward the stairs together.

About thirty seconds later, security arrived by way of the elevator. They immediately hoisted the drink machine off Alan and let it fall to the floor.

"You," one man said when they were finished. "You jumped into the fountain. That's not allowed."

"I was running away from *your* hotel's manager, who was trying to kill me," I snapped. "I was protecting myself."

"Alan? He was trying to kill you? I find that hard to believe," one of the security guards said, raising an eyebrow. He was bald, about six-two, with the build of a guy who was totally a linebacker on his high school football team.

"Well, his gun's lying in the hallway down there. Do you really think I decided to pretend your water feature was Splash Mountain all by myself? No. I was running for my life. By the way, you might want to call him an ambulance."

"She's telling the truth," Dot said. "He attacked her. I saw it."

The security guards still looked skeptical. "But he's the hotel manager," one said, while the other pulled out his phone and began to dial for help.

"Yes, no one in a position of power has ever done anything bad before," I said, rolling my eyes. "Look, this lady that I don't know is telling you I was attacked. I was just defending myself."

"Do I look like the kind of person who would lie to you?" Dot asked, giving the security guard her most innocent look.

Finally, he sighed. "Fine. Okay, look. I'm calling for backup. Hold on."

The man got onto his radio for a bit and then pressed his palms into his eyes. Obviously, this wasn't the kind of situation he had been expecting to respond to on his shift tonight.

"Did you say there was a gun?" he asked.

I nodded. "It should be down the hallway there somewhere."

The guard went and looked and returned a minute later, carrying it in a tissue. "Okay. I don't want this just lying around. I'm going to have to call the police."

"You might also want to call the FBI agents who are on the case about the guy who was murdered. Your manager there? He's the one who killed him."

The security guard swore. "Just when you think it's going to be a normal shift without anything weird happening."

Chapter 23

The next few hours passed in a bit of a blur, and not entirely due to the probable concussion I was dealing with.

I asked the security guard to grab Lucy, the CIA agent, from the wedding reception downstairs. I told her everything, and she accompanied Alan in the ambulance, promising that if he tried to escape, he wasn't leaving it alive. I had no doubt that she meant it.

After that, everything began to go a bit hazy.

"Charlie?" Dot said. "You need to go to the hospital. Come on. We're going to take you."

The last thing I remembered was being helped into the back of Rosie's CR-V and her driving like a bat out of hell toward Kahului.

I WOKE UP IN THE HOSPITAL TO THE SOUND OF ZOE

arguing with somebody. I didn't open my eyes. My head hurt like crazy.

"I don't care what your credentials say. She's resting, and you can't talk to her."

"We're with the FBI. We can talk to whoever we want." That was Agent Forrester's voice. "Wake her up. We need to get a statement."

"First of all, that's not how science works. I can't just 'wake her up,' as you say, because her body is sleeping so it can heal itself. Secondly, I took an oath to do no harm. Even if I could wake her up, I wouldn't do it. You can wait for her to wake up naturally, and if you're going to insist on abusing my patient, I'll have security escort you off the premises."

Agent Forrester scoffed. "Right. Like those rent-a-cops can do anything."

"Maybe they can't, but I can," Jake's voice said suddenly. Why was he here? "And unlike Dr. Morgan here, I never took an oath to do no harm. No one is saying you can't talk to Charlie. But you can't put her health in jeopardy to do it."

"Was that a threat? Did you just threaten a federal agent?"

"It was more like a promise," Jake replied. "You threatened a resident of this island."

"Why do I get the feeling she's more than just a resident to you?"

"Okay, this is enough. Agent, I need you to leave the room now to let my patient rest. Are you going to do it on your own, or does Detective Llewelyn here have to escort you out?"

I could practically feel the staredown I knew was happening, and a moment later, Agent Forrester's voice replied, "Fine. I'll go. But the moment she wakes up, I want to be told. I need to take her statement."

"As soon as she's cleared medically, I'll have you alerted," Zoe said, her tone shutting down any idea of the conversation going further.

"You do that," Agent Forrester snarled. A moment later, I heard a door slam shut.

"Asshole," Zoe muttered under her breath. "Like I'm going to wake up Charlie just so she can give a witness statement."

"Glad you've got my back," I said weakly, opening my eyes.

Zoe and Jake both turned to look at me. Zoe rushed to my side, pulling out one of those mini flashlights and shining it into my eyes.

"Ugh. I would have pretended to still be asleep if I knew you were going to do that."

"Sorry, but I have to see how your pupils are reacting to the light."

"Badly. The answer is badly. What happened?"

"You're concussed. You must have hit your head at some point."

With difficulty, my mind turned back to what had happened at the hotel. "Oh, yeah. Probably a few times, actually. A concussion makes a lot of sense."

"That's why you're in this room. I want to limit the amount of stimuli you're exposed to until I can further assess how you're doing. You're going to go in for a brain scan in about ten minutes; I want to check for internal bleeding just to be safe."

"What happened to Alan? Is he dead?" I asked.

"He's in surgery. He has a broken leg, and his spleen burst when the vending machine landed on him. He also has a cut on his head, but nothing major."

"That means he'll live?"

"Based on the information I was given, it's likely. I assume he's the killer?"

I nodded. "Yes. We figured it out before we left. He ghosted Rosie, and we were just going to bail on the whole idea when he injected me with something. I passed out, woke up in a hotel room covered in plastic sheeting, and escaped. He tried coming after me, but I still got away. Eventually, Dot managed to push the vending machine on top of him."

"Statistically, they're more dangerous than sharks," Zoe pointed out.

"Nice try. I'm still not going to enjoy the ocean."

"Dot phoned me while Rosie was driving you here," Jake explained. "She said that the feds were probably going to want to speak to you and that they were probably going to be pretty pissed because a spook took the suspect away first. She actually said the word 'spook.' Were you actually involved in a case that's got not only the feds but the CIA mixed up in it?"

I nodded. "Yeah. Rex Thunder was trying to sell Alan a thumb drive with a bunch of sensitive info on it. The CIA were in on it, trying to catch the buyer, and when Rex was murdered, they were the ones who called the FBI in."

"That explains a lot."

"Unfortunately, the feds also had no idea Alan was the killer. I don't know how this is going to play out."

"You don't have to worry about that right now," Zoe said. "You need to rest."

"Where are Dot and Rosie?"

"They left," Jake said. "They wanted me to let you know they send their love, but they wanted to stay out of it as much as possible. They said you'd know what that meant."

I nodded. "Good. I'll get in touch with them when I get out of here."

"Are you up for speaking with the federal agents?" Zoe asked.

"Yeah, I think so."

"I'll stay with you while you do. I don't trust Agent Forrester at all, especially not when you're in a vulnerable state," Jake said with a scowl.

"I'm fine," I said. "Believe me."

"I'm staying, and that's final."

"Okay," I said. I didn't want to admit it, but a part of me was glad Jake was going to be here.

"Right. I'll be back to check on you in a little bit," Zoe said. She left.

About two minutes later, Agent Forrester entered the room. His eyes landed on Jake, and he glared at him. "This is a private conversation."

"He stays," I replied.

Agent Forrester scowled. "I don't like having a regular police officer here."

"Well, I don't like you, so none of us are happy," I replied.

Jake chuckled lightly next to me, and Agent Forrester let out a heavy sigh as if this was totally not what he'd signed up for.

"Fine. Listen, I know what you told Lucy: that Alan, the hotel manager, is the man who killed Rex. Is that true?"

"Yes."

"Can you run me through how you know that?"

"Sure. Are you going to arrest him for the murder?"

Agent Forrester scowled again. "We're not being allowed anywhere near him. The CIA have decided they're taking over and that they get first bite at this particular apple. And I know how this goes. Alan will disappear and never be heard from again. That's their M.O. So I'm not thrilled. I want him to face justice for this murder, which means I'm still going to need a statement from you."

"Are you going to charge him with my attempted murder if you get the chance?" I asked.

"No. That's not my case. It would fall to the local cops. So can you tell me everything?"

I ran through what I knew, repeating to Agent Forrester what I'd found out, changing some pertinent details to make it sound as if I had been a lone wolf on this case. Dot and Rosie's names never came up at all.

When I got to the end, Agent Forrester raised an eyebrow. "You figured all this out by yourself?"

"I sure did."

"That seems unlikely to me."

"Why? Because you couldn't do it?"

"Yes. Exactly. I'm a trained field agent. You're just a P.I."

"Well, maybe the FBI need to be more particular about who they take in." Jake chuckled next to me. "But I'm telling you, that's how it went."

Agent Forrester still looked skeptical. "If you say so. Where is the thumb drive now?"

"I don't know," I said. Technically, it wasn't a lie. Rosie probably still had it on her, but I couldn't be certain. "I don't know what's happened to my phone, either. I would ask Alan about it."

"Right. Well, that's the CIA's problem now. Okay, that's all I need from you." Agent Forrester stood up and left.

"He's certainly got some bedside manner," Jake said.

I laughed. "No kidding. Thanks for staying with me."

"Uh, yeah, no problem," Jake said, running a hand through his hair. "I figured with the feds around, you never know, right?"

"Yeah, for sure."

"So, uh, I guess I'll get going. Unless you need me to stay."

"I should be fine. I'll see you later?"

"Yeah. Back at home. I'll be around."

With that, Jake stood up and left, shooting me one last glance before leaving the room. I tried to ignore the slight pang in my chest that told me I wanted him to stay.

I was just feeling vulnerable because I was in the hospital. That was definitely it.

As I was being wheeled back to my room by an attendant after getting my brain scanned to check for a bleed, I spotted Lucy in the hallway.

"Hey, Lucy," I called out to her.

She looked up. "You're the P.I. Heather hired," she said. "The one Alan just tried to kill."

"That's me," I said. "Can you walk back with me to my room?"

"Alan's still in surgery. That's fine."

Lucy followed me, and when I was settled once more and the attendant had left, she spoke. "So, what is this about?"

"What's going to happen to Alan after he goes through his surgery? You know, assuming he survives and all."

"I'm afraid I can't tell you that. It's classified information."

"He's going to go on trial?"

Lucy laughed coldly. "Honey, we're the CIA. We don't do trials."

"All right, fine. He's going to disappear into a hole in the middle of nowhere."

"I can't tell you."

"Oh, come on. I basically handed you this guy on a silver platter. I heard you talking to those two FBI agents. You didn't have a clue who Rex's contact was.

So fine, don't tell me what's going to happen to Alan, but answer some other questions for me. You at least owe me that. How did you get into contact with Rex? Did he come to you, or did you find him?"

Lucy looked uncomfortably around the room. "Where's your phone?"

"Haven't seen it since Alan jabbed me with something to knock me unconscious. It's probably long gone. Believe me, given my history, I've taken to appreciating the service iCloud provides."

Lucy gave me an appraising look then pulled out her own phone, tapped away at it for a minute, and then nodded.

"Okay, there are no recording devices in this room. Nothing I say leaves here. I will deny telling you anything if it's ever reported."

"Understood."

"Rex came onto our radar about a year ago. It turned out he was selling sensitive information to people overseas, information he was getting by bribing the right people. Given that he was a property developer, a lot of the interactions he had with others seemed completely innocent, so it took us a long time to realize that was where the information was coming from. We waited until we'd gathered enough information on him and then confronted him. He immediately flipped and offered to work as a double agent. He told us he would be meeting his main contact to sell some more data at his daughter's wedding and offered to help us with a sting operation."

"Who was the ultimate buyer?"

"An energy tycoon working out of Dubai," Lucy replied. "I'm not at liberty to share any more than that."

"Right, that makes sense given what was on that drive."

"Do you have it?" Lucy asked sternly.

I shook my head. "No. I think it faced the same fate as my phone. Or maybe Alan still has it. That might be why he didn't want to follow me into the fountain." I was getting pretty good at thinking on my feet.

"Well, I'm sure I'll find out when he wakes up."

"Was he working alone? Rex, I mean."

"Yes. We looked into everyone else in his life. Family, friends, business associates. Nothing else came up, and he swore to us up and down that he was a lone wolf. I believe him."

"Okay. Now, tell me Alan's never going to be a free man ever again."

Lucy barked out a laugh. "You don't have to worry about that. Even if we ever decide we're done with him, we'll dump him into the laps of the feds. Not that I expect that to happen anytime soon. I'm sure my boss will get an angry phone call from the head of their field office, but that's how the cookie crumbles. They only got called in because we can't be seen openly investigating crimes on US soil and because we wanted to keep Rex's work for us secret."

"Good to know."

"How long have you been working as a P.I.?"

"A few months."

"Go figure. You're better than half those whiz kids

we recruit out of Stanford and Harvard. If you ever decide you want a real fun career, come work for us. I'll put in a good word for you."

"What do I do, just flash a Bat-Signal in the sky that says 'CIA HIRE ME' and wait for the black helicopters to show up?"

Lucy snorted. "Heh. Something like that. There's a website these days. You apply there. And here's my card." She reached into her pocket and pulled out a plain white card with her name, phone number and an innocuous-looking email address.

"Well, thanks for the offer, but I think Maui has enough excitement for me for now. If I change my mind one day, I'll let you know. Good luck with Alan."

Lucy headed toward the door. "Take care, Charlotte."

And with that, she was gone. Given who was involved, I was pretty sure those were all the answers I was ever going to get. Heather's name hadn't come up at all; the CIA obviously just believed her to be an innocent wife. All the loose ends were tied up.

Well, except one.

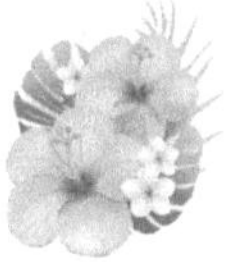

Epilogue

Two days later, Olivia and I were sharing a beer at the picnic table in her front yard. Egg McMuffin was curled up into a ball on her bed near the front door, snoring away, the tennis ball only inches from her nose.

I'd just finished telling Olivia the story of Samantha and Sean, and how she wasn't being abused, she was actually running a robbery ring targeting men who were away from their wives.

When I was finished, Olivia let out a low whistle. "Damn. And here I thought I had good instincts. I like Samantha. She seemed so normal."

"Well, it's not like she had 'My boyfriend and I make our money running a crime ring robbing tourists' stamped on her forehead," I said with a shrug. "I bet a lot of people have had casual conversations with bad people without knowing about it. Even the Zodiac Killer had to get groceries at some point."

Olivia chuckled. "Is that supposed to make me feel better?"

"I'm just saying, this isn't on you. You couldn't have known. And really, if you hadn't assumed the worst and brought me in on this, they never would have been caught. It's really thanks to you that they were, ultimately."

"I'll take that credit. Even if I had the reason entirely wrong. That's insane. Who does that?"

I shrugged. "Some people just do not have any sense of right and wrong."

"No kidding. But wow. Armed robbery?"

"Does it really count as armed when all you have is a twenty-dollar Taser you bought from a shady website that probably stole your credit card information?"

Olivia snorted. "I'm pretty sure it does. How many victims did they have?"

"I'm not sure. I think Jake said at least ten, but I imagine there's no way to ever know for certain. Either way, it was a lot."

"I'm just glad they're not out there anymore. Still, I can't believe I didn't see it at all. I feel like an idiot."

"I mean, I don't want to tell you how to feel, but I'm absolutely about to do just that. Not only is this not your fault—it's not like you and Samantha were best friends—but it's because of you that they were stopped. Think of yourself as a hero, not a moron. I think that's good life advice no matter the situation."

"You know what? You're right. I *am* a hero. And heroes deserve another beer," she said, cracking open the top of another Bud Light.

I was driving back into town a little while later when I got a text from Heather.

I need to see you, and preferably your two friends as well. Can we meet?

I arranged for Heather to come to my apartment and texted Dot and Rosie letting them know what was going on. An hour later, Heather knocked on the door.

I opened the door and motioned for her to enter. Heather looked older and wearier than she had just a few days earlier. Coco ran up and sniffed her leg, and Heather reached down to pet her. Thrilled to have gotten some attention, Coco then ran over to Rosie and hopped up next to her on the couch and lay down.

"Thank you for seeing me," she said. "All three of you. I wanted to thank you in person for finding the man who killed Rex. Charlie explained to me over the phone that the CIA has him, and there won't be a trial. That's for the best, I think."

"Why did you need us here?" Rosie asked.

Heather pressed her lips together. "Am I to assume your name is Rosemary?" she said in response.

"If it is?"

Heather reached into her purse and pulled out an envelope. "I found this among Rex's things when I was going through and packing all our stuff. It was hidden behind the seam of his luggage."

I caught a glimpse of it as she walked across the room and handed it to Rosie. It had her name on it.

"Thank you," Rosie said.

"I don't know what this is about. I don't know how

you knew my husband, but please tell me you had nothing to do with his death."

"I promise you, I didn't. I haven't spoken to your husband in decades. Since before you even met him."

Heather's shoulders relaxed slightly. "Thank you. I don't know your story, although I can guess it would be remarkably similar to mine. But I appreciate you telling me. I wonder how he found out about you."

"I don't know," Rosie replied. "I never once spoke to him after I… left."

"Understood. I just wanted you to have this before I head back to New York. And I wanted to thank you all. For everything. Oh, and this is for you, Charlie. I hope it's satisfactory." Heather handed me an envelope, gave a single curt nod and left.

Rosie's fingers ran along the edge of the envelope, and she stared at it. "His handwriting is still the same," she said.

"Well, what are you waiting for?" Dot asked. "Open it."

"Dot!" I said. "Even I know this is the kind of thing Rosie might want to do in private."

Rosie smiled at me. "Thank you. But Dot is right. I'll open it here. After all, I think we all want the answers that may be contained in this letter."

"If it starts getting smutty, I'm leaving," I warned them.

"I'm not," Dot said excitedly, bouncing lightly up and down in her spot.

"Oh, I have one other question," I said quickly. "What happened to the thumb drive?"

"Destroyed," Rosie said. "After we dropped you off at the hospital, we took care of it. The data on it is gone forever. We thought that was safest."

"Good call," I said.

Dot and I watched as Rosie slowly opened the envelope, the sound of the paper tearing the only noise in the room. Rosie pulled out a single sheet of paper. Dot and I watched as she skimmed it silently. When she was finished, she stood and handed it to Dot.

"If you don't mind, I'm just going to go outside for a little bit," Rosie said. "I need to gather my thoughts. I'll be back in a while."

"Take all the time you need," I replied. "I'll be here. We both will."

When Rosie left, Dot read the letter herself then passed it silently to me.

The paper was thick and heavy; this wasn't a sheet of ordinary printer paper. The writing was elegant but with the slightest tremble in the lettering that so often accompanied writing by someone of advanced age.

Rosemary,

I apologize for not getting in touch sooner. If you've received this letter, then my last visit to this beautiful island has been completed, and I will likely never return again.

I saw your face again for the first time three years ago, and though decades had passed, I was as certain of your identity as I was of my own middle name. It was you. Standing in the market, choosing the perfect mango.

And at that moment, my heart stopped. I longed to go to you, to tell you how I felt. Even after all these years, I never forgot you. I was married, through work, to a woman named Heather. She's a lot like you. I think the two of you could be friends if you ever met.

But you were my first true love, and a part of my heart has always been reserved for you, even after all these years.

I followed you; saw your license plate. I looked you up. Your name changed. You didn't go for Eleanor after all. You would have thought it imprudent. That's because you were always smarter than me that way. Always more careful.

I'm glad you got out. I'm glad you lived your own life, eating mangoes in this paradise for decades. It's a better life than what they had planned for us, I'm sure.

I simply hope you're happy.

Every time I came here, I asked myself if I was doing the right thing. Perhaps I should have revealed myself to you. Sent you a sign that the man you once loved on the other side of the world was here, only a few miles away. But I admit to cowardice, Eleanor. I feared you would push me away, the same way you pushed everything else from your life back then. I wouldn't have blamed you. I couldn't have blamed you. I know exactly what it takes.

But I also know this: the instant I laid eyes on you, for the first time in years, I knew in my heart that you were the one. You were the woman I was meant to love with every ounce of my being. And I did love you. I do love you. And I will continue to do so until the day I die, even knowing that I will never see you again.

So it became enough that you were here. Every time I landed on Maui, I knew your spirit was close, and that was enough. But now, my time on this island has come to an end. I'm not sure what form the rest of my life will take, but I wanted you to know.

I loved you then, and I love you now.

We grew old together, even if we were not together.

Perhaps in another life, we will be given that privilege.

But for now, know that a piece of my heart is with you always.

Take care, Eleanor.

Rex

Book 6 - Kalikimaka Killer: Christmas in Hawaii is all surfing Santa Claus, palm trees strung up with lights and… murder?

It's the most wonderful time of the year on Maui, although not so much for one of Zoe's patients. Zoe is convinced the woman was murdered, despite her death being ruled accidental, but the police won't listen to her so she goes to Charlie for help.

The two of them, along with Dot and Rosie, set out to get justice for Zoe's patient. But what initially looks like it might be a simple case quickly becomes complicated, and Charlie finds herself in more danger than cookies left out on Christmas Eve.

Oh, and is that Jake standing under the mistletoe?

All Charlie wants for Christmas is to catch a murderer. That's not too much for a girl to ask for, is it?

Click here to pre-order Kalikimaka Killer now (coming November 29th, 2022)

About the Author

Jasmine Webb is a thirty-something who lives in the mountains most of the year, dreaming of the beach. When she's not writing stories you can find her chasing her old dog around, hiking up moderately-sized hills, or playing Pokemon Go.

Sign up for Jasmine's newsletter to be the first to find out about new releases here: http://www.authorjasminewebb.com/newsletter

You can also connect with her on other social media here:

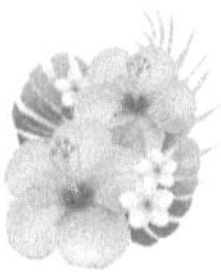

A Note from the Author

Hi! I just wanted to say thank you for reading Hibiscus Homicide. I really hope you enjoyed this book, because I had a blast writing it.

If you'd like to help other readers find this book as well, please consider leaving a review on Amazon or Goodreads, or on whatever platform you purchased this book.

I have plenty of stories for Charlie and friends coming up in the future, and you can preorder Kalikimaka Killer, the sixth book in the series. That's coming in late November, perfect to get you into that Christmas mood!

Until next time, I hope you're able to enjoy some sunshine, and that every book you read brings you unhinged joy.

Jasmine

Also by Jasmine Webb

Charlotte Gibson Mysteries

Aloha Alibi

Maui Murder

Beachside Bullet

Pina Colada Poison

Hibiscus Homicide

Kalikimaka Killer (coming November 2022)

www.ingramcontent.com/pod-product-compliance
Lightning Source LLC
Chambersburg PA
CBHW030529310726
48979CB00010B/1844/J

9781777799380